The Last Voyage
Of the Ghost Cartel
James Marquis

THE LAST VOYAGE OF THE GHOST CARTEL

James Marquis

CONTENTS

FORWARD

$\mathcal{T}$he "Last Voyage of the Ghost Cartel" is just that. The author takes the reader from the jungles of Vietnam, (1968 Vietnam War Love Story) to the Caribbean Sea (Marquis Cartel & Revenge of the Marquis Cartel), to the South Pacific, in the "Ghost Cartel" which is headquartered in the "King of Tonga". Then back to the Caribbean in "The Last Voyage," for a series of drug seizures, mutiny, death, love, and passion that the reader will be introduced to through the minds and action of the only gay cartel in the world. Staffed with thousands of Jamaican Thugs, and specialized teams from KENYA, who together pledge their "life to the Cartel, then to their pardner, and fight to their death to complete the cartel's mission".

Revealed are the integrated plans put in place to close down the world's largest cartel and its only remaining members took voyage on the "Ghost Ships", to evade detection from Drug Enforcement Agency, F.B.I., and other federal agencies. With billions of dollars at risk, they found a way to avoid arrest, while the financial world recognized them as one of the biggest money laundering cartels abound.

"Treason" in the cartel world brings on its own special challenges. Love and heartbreak can chatter the most tender relationship. One treasonist individual can break a person's heart for years or open it up to a new adventure, as detailed in the "Last Voyage."

"The Last Voyage" reveals the emotional closure of the **"Marquis Cartel"** and its continued search for renewed passion.

ONE YEAR LATER
4:05 A.M.

At 4:05 A.M. The Saturday before Thanksgiving, Captain Oliver along with his First Officer Wayne were now preparing the Tito V or the Ghost Ship, as it is referred to, to depart Monck's Bay in Christchurch, New Zealand. After clearing the yacht club entrance Cpt. Oliver set a course due North to the cartel's headquarters on the Island of Tonga, a 1700-mile voyage.

Chef Jeffery along with his sidekick Timothy had made provisions for Thanksgiving at sea, as the voyage would take a week to reach their Tong headquarters. King, wrapped in the arms of his newfound love the "Black Falcon '', as he referred to him. King felt the motion of the ocean, coming not from between his legs but rather from the force of the powerful MTU 4000 engines of the 250' TITO V. He said to Winston, "we are on the move, let's enjoy the view of the ghost leaving Monck Bay. They both slipped into their silk robes and went to the office with its 360 degrees panoramic view. Once inside Winston, 12 years younger than King, took him by the waist and set him on his lap and hugged him as if it were his last.

Once at sea Chef Jeffery started preparations for an early morning brunch to celebrate their first morning under way. All plans were made for a leisurely trip to Tonga. The rest of the crew and cartel staff on board were relaxing in their staterooms, kicking back enjoying themselves to the fullest. Capt. Oliver put the yacht on "automatic pilot" and put his arms around Wayne and drew him near and planted a juice kiss on his lips. Oliver and Wayne had become an indescribable team since they joined forces many months ago.

Oliver, Wayne's senior by a little over ten years, had the "bull" stamina of an 18-year-old. With that amount of energy, he kept Wayne fully challenged to meet all of Oliver's advances. Wayne's muscled build kept Oliver ever ready to intermix their pleasures.

David appears in the office with his silk robe tied tight around his waist. His first comment was, "it is sure nice to be under way". "New Zealand was nice but it is so busy and I prefer the open sea, as it provides a degree of protection while we travel." All three of them stood up and walked over to the office window as the Ghost Ship cleared the yacht harbor and the eastern coastline of NZ was fading into the western horizon.

Chef Jeffery laid out a massive brunch on the second deck and Tim made Mimosas and Bloody Mary's for all the willing participants.

After they finished eating the cartel members discussed the successful operation that Ian & Cyprian formed in NZ.

A.J.

*D*uring Ian's & Cyprain's first four months in operation they collected $8.5 million in net revenue. They had established a relationship with an accountant, like David, with a smaller cartel, that unknowingly gave them leads on their cartel shipments arriving in NZ. The guy's name was A.J, about 5'8", dreadlocks to his shoulders, and extremely handsome. King didn't know much about the cartel and never heard about the relationship A.J. had with Ian & Cyprian.

Ian was first to meet A.J. at a private cocktail party hosted by a large cocaine dealer in Christchurch. As weeks passed, using his "black magic", Ian invited A.J. to join him & Cyprian for a dinner on board the Tito V. When A.J. arrived, he was taken back as to the grandeur of the 250' floating five star hotel. His body language communicated distrust and he was extremely nervous, despite the fact he had known Ian for almost a month.

All three gathered in the main saloon of the yacht. The steward appeared to take drink orders and A.J. said, "do you have anything strong"? Ian looked at Cyprian with concern in his eyes. Ian spoke up and said, "what is it that you desire?" A.J. without hesitation he replied, "a double Hennessy's on the rocks and then if you feel up to it, I will let you both enjoy what many people say, is a beautiful smooth body of a Polynesian man." Cyprian stood up and said "let's have drinks in our master suite.

Setting in the living area of the suite, drinks arrived. A.J. had excused himself to the bathroom for a quick hot shower leaving Ian & Cyprian alone in the living room. They both looked at each other and laughed. They have been victim to this sex play several times over the years.

One is not to be trusted that comes aboard and desires sex with the ghosts. Caution is now their first concern.

A.J. came out of the bathroom completely nude. I&C (Ian & Cyprian) stared in disbelief. It was true. He looks like a Polynesian god with his light chocolate skin, dark brown eyes, braided hair to the neckline, soft facial features, and so much hanging between his legs, who could resist? A.J. walking with this Harlem swag, sat down on the velvet sofa facing I&C, and spread his legs. His pubic hair had been recently shaved.

Ian, who had known A.J. the longest asked: "what is it that you want from us"? Protection was his reply. He went on to say, "I know that you have been using me for information on drug shipments, and I have gladly funneled them to you. There is going to be a time when my tips to your cartel are detected and my life will be in danger. I need protection and better, yet I need to get out of NZ. In return, I will provide you with all the drug warehouses, shipment schedules, and dates. A.J. said, even onboard this vessel, I need to keep a low profile, one never knows the eyes and ears that are out there. TITO V is known by all who are in the drug business. A.J., no matter how handsome you are and the cartel connections you have, to gain passage on any of the Ghost Ships, you must be approved of by the one all-powerful King, the leader of the Marquis Cartel and the Ghost Cartel. I suggest you don't shave your pubes any more just in case you just happen to meet and or be interviewed by King. He finds that area shaved extremely non-masculine.

During King and David's visit to NZ to check out I&C newly formed operation, Ian told King about A.J., and that $8 million in profit had come from tips from

A.J. and accountant for a smaller cartel operating out of southern NZ. Ian told King about the conversation that he had with A.J. and the deal he offered in exchange for passage off the island.

King did not trust anyone who would betray their cartel to get into another cartel to save their own life. Once a ghost, always a ghost till death. That was his cartel's motto and sworn belief. For any member who cannot live by that rule, is not allowed, or considered to become a member of King's cartel. King told Ian that A.J. needs to prove himself loyal to the ghost before any consideration is given to his wellbeing. I&C contacted A.J. and requested that he meet them at the Del Mar Club, where most of the well-healed dealers hang out.

During the meeting, Ian explained to A.J. that it will take more than a naked body to gain access to their organization. King approves all new members to the ghost cartel and your willingness to turn on your own cartel sets a standard of distrust. Would you do the same to the ghost?

A.J. did not quite understand why they would give up all the information on drug shipments in exchange for not getting him out of NZ. He had made them over $8 million dollars, that should buy his way into any operation. The Ghost Cartel, he thought, must be well funded and highly skilled to maintain its hold on the South Pacific Islands. He thought there must be another way to get off this dangerous island.

About a day out of Christchurch they were fifty miles due east of Wellington, located on the north island of NZ. King received a call on the secure line from Ian, at their Little Port operation in South NZ. He informed King that he had just received a call from A.J. telling him that two cartels had gotten together and dispatched 15 "go-boats" to take over the TITO V. Their goal was to destroy King and David plus the entire crew and cartel members on board.

The TITO V carried 2 "go-boats" that they could launch at any time plus the yacht was armed with state-of-the-art weapon systems that reached over 100 miles in any direction. Simon, head of security, was immediately informed of the pending attack. He sounded the alert. All crew and cartel members reported to their defensive stations.

Simon decided not to lower their 'go-boats' into the water as 15 to 2 aren't favorable odds for a water-to-water battle. Instead, he chose to use all of the yacht's anti-boat missiles which could knock out incoming watercraft miles before they got within firing range of the Ghost Ship. Now it was a waiting game. On the radar of the Ghost Ship, it was revealed that numerous watercrafts had just entered the TITO V's area. Simon, with his seal team training, programmed rockets to be launched at 5 second intervals for the next 2 minutes. Only two rockets missed their target.

Simon gave orders to lower their 'go-boats' to give chase, as the last two attack craft were now on retreat. The TITO V's boats were so powerful that they overtook the retreating craft within minutes. The Ghost Cartel members left the once threatening gang bobbing in the water of the South Pacific and their boats sinking to the ocean floor.

Once the attack was neutralized King put a call into Ian & Cyprian location and thanked them for the information about the attack and to have A.J. catch a helicopter to the TITO V. King wanted to talk to him, in person, about joining the Ghost Cartel. Just the break A.J. was hoping for.

King, Winston, and David were in the office of the Ghost Ship when the helicopter touched down. A.J. stepped out of the plane and walked across the deck, not revealing that swagger as before. He was smartly dressed and had a polished smile on his face. He had only heard rumors about King of the Jamaican Cartel who is now the leader of the largest cartel both in the Caribbean and South Pacific. Most of all rumors were, he was feared and would kill without mercy. A.J. was scared shit-less but he couldn't show it.

When he walked into the office where King, Winston and David were sitting, the first words out of his mouth were "thank you for saving my life." King was taken back by his pleading comment. King replied, "I think we owe you the thank you." A.J. said I can't go back to NZ, my life is incomplete danger after tipping you off about the cartel attack. There were only a handful of trusted members of the cartels involved who knew of the attack and I was one of them. It won't take them long to figure out that I was the snitch and then I am dead. There is no place to hide in or around New Zealand.

King was taken back by how handsome he was. A.J. had a look about him that was so smooth and sexy. King was wondering if he was using his looks to get what he wanted or was sincere about leaving the cartel in NZ to save his own skin. Winston asked him if he had a companion? A.J. said he had a girlfriend/wife. He would her give up in a flash to save his life and join the ghost, but of course his coloring is not very dark. The light milk chocolate doesn't fit the mold of the Ghost Cartel but some of its members are lighter skinned, but they often take a back seat to the "Executive-Service" cartel members from Kenya.

A.J. said, "I will do anything to escape NZ and prove my worth to your organization. I am a CPA and know all drug shipping routes in the South Pacific. King spoke up, "have you ever toured a 250' yacht? A.J. replied, "I have never been on or seen anything this big or beautiful in my entire life. King said, then follow me, you're in for a surprise.

As they toured the TITO V, A.J. was introduced to so many of the crew and staff on board he was overwhelmed by their black beauty. The Kenya men were so sexy he thought to himself how he could ever compare to any of them. When they entered the master suite Winston was sitting on the velvet sofa in his silk polo rob. A.J. looked around in amazement as to the size of the suite. King shut the door with a bang and headed to the bathroom, emerging a short time later in his robe.

What are you doing still standing there mystified A.J., King said, "jump into the shower, there is a white terry cloth robe hanging behind the door for you. When you're finished, join Winston and I in the living room for drinks".

A.J. shower ever crack and crevices he had. He said that he would do anything not to go back to N.Z., he may have to prove it to the leader of the most powerful cartel. When he emerged from the bathroom, he looked darker, wrapped in the white robe. King asked him what he wanted to drink? His reply, Hennessy on the rocks, makes it a double, I think I may need it...

King replied, "You're saved by our relationship." Winston and I are in a very comfortable relationship, you sexually pose no interest to us. I am more concerned with how you physically look so we know how you will fit in with our gay cartel and how comfortable you will be doing it?

When was the last time you had any type of passion with a man? A.J. replied, "never in reality, only in fantasy, which I am looking forward to fulfilling." King replied, "our cartel is all reality". Have a seat in the chair across from us A.J., now open that robe let's see what a creole and Polynesian man looks like.

After a long intense look, Winston looked at King and said, "that is too beautiful to pass up". King replied, As soon as those pubes grow out "I think we found our secret weapon". Let's enjoy our drinks and get to know each other. King went on to say, "our entire cartel is built on the foundation of protecting the cartel 1st, your pardner 2nd and your life is last." A.J. listened as Winston and King shared their softer side while trying to get a response from him, but he kept everything close to his chest. In about an hour King called the Chief Steward to have A.J. assigned a stateroom.

THANKSGIVING

A Thanksgiving dinner was laid out buffet style in the dining room of the Ghost Ship. Chef Jeffery made sure that the Turkey and Ham plus all the trimmings were enough for the entire staff and crew on board. When the dining hour approached couples began to arrive showing off the strong bonds that were in place on the TITO V.

King and Winston were at one end of the table and David sat alone at the other end. Sixteen chairs were filled, eight on each side, with the ghost and crew of the TITO V. The last person to walk into the dining room was the new kid on the block, A.J. He smiled and greeted everyone cordially. He said, "Is there a seat left for me"? David was first to speak up. "There is an empty seat next to me." A.J. looked at David remembering him from the brief encounter, in the office, when he arrived. A.J. thanked David then pulled a chair up to the end of the table and the Steward prepared a place setting for him.

The staff around the table were very interested in the new person sitting to the left of David. King had made a brief introduction which involved A.J. contribution to Ian & Cyprian's operation in NZ and the information that he leaked about the most recent cartel attack that they foiled off the coastline of Wellington. The question-and-answer period began and lasted through dinner. The ghosts were more than interested in A.J.'s reason for turning on his cartel. That is a sacred trust that a member should never break. A.J., took all of the badgering in stride and then he got up from his chair and started walking around the table. As he did, he explained, "the answer is very simply, if I didn't turn on my former cartel, **none** of you would be celebrating this beautiful Thanksgiving meal together". Let's eat, drink, and be merry.

After the exquisite dinner was finished, they gathered on the aft deck for drinks. King and Winston excused themselves and went to the man cave to plan for their arrival in Tonga, which would be in less than 30 hours. One more glorious night at sea then the Ghost Ship will be docked at their Tonga headquarters.' David, with his innocent mind, sat down next to A.J.

and inquired as to his position at his former cartel. He went on to say that he thought it was much like David's, planning drug hits, movement of money to avoid detection by the DEA and IRS of their country, and to make sure all staff and crew were paid. A.J. said, I did all of those things, but I had to be on the lookout for larger cartels planning a takeover of our cartel. Every day it was more dangerous than the day or week before because cartels in NZ were growing faster than drugs can be shipped in. I knew it was only a matter of time and we would be eliminated. It's called survival of the fittest. I did only what I had to do to survive.

As evening drew near, the sunset on the western horizon was so red and fiery one could only hear the TITO V cutting the waves of the blue waters of the South Pacific. Most of the members had now paired off in their staterooms to enjoy their final night at sea, leaving only A.J. and David who had now relocated to the massive main saloon. Once inside David asks A.J. if he would like a drink and of course he replied to a Hennessy on the rocks, David had a diet coke.

As they sat across from one another on the richly upholstered leather sofas, David informed A.J. that he was the only founding member of the Marquis Cartel that is alive. King had joined the cartel several years ago and was the companion of the other founding member who succumbed to cancer. David also informed him that King protects him with a vengeance and to always keep that information first and foremost in his mind if you want to live long on the ghost ship.

David got up off of the sofa and said, "it's well past my bedtime, we will be arriving in Tonga tomorrow morning so I need to be well rested to begin planning for all the money transfers that I need to complete while we are in port". A.J. said, "do you think I can tag along with you so I understand how you minuplite all your hidden wealth? David replied, " that will be up to King". David retired to his suite. Once inside he was thinking about how quickly A.J. expressed an interest in getting to know more information about ghost financial affairs than any of the long-time members. He will give King a heads up so he can address the issue with A.J.

TONGA

*T*he Ghost Ship, in all of its pristine glory, motored into the harbor of Tonga right on schedule early the seventh morning at sea after leaving NZ. Winston's Lieutenants were dockside to tie up the yacht and welcome their leader back after weeks at sea. King, Winston, and David were first to disembark, and they went to the office where all of the records and computers were located. King, along with Winston's 1st Lieutenant toured the cutting room, where all of the incoming shipments are broken down and repackaged for distribution. The remaining crew reunited with old friends and others went into town to enjoy the beauty of the Polynesian men.

Alone, A.J. went into the central city to seek out any information he could about males for hire, as he needed to practice up on his newly expressed lifestyle. As late evening was approaching, he nosed out a mixed gay bar in the drug triangle of the city. It was seedy, but he needed information, and that's all. He approached a guy sitting at the end of the bar who was very dark skinned. Obviously not born of Polynesian blood, he inquired where he could locate a gay bathhouse? The guy immediately introduced himself as Emmitt, from the Tahitian Islands. Emmitt asked A.J. wouldn't you rather join me in a beautiful home rather than a dirty bathhouse for the evening? A.J. thought for only a second and said that sounds inviting, may I join you for a drink? What's your pleasure? Hennessy on the rocks, make it a double, it is going to be a very interesting night for both of us.

As A.J. walked alongside Emmitt down a tree lined street in the richly populated part of Nuku'alofa the capital of Tonga he was thinking there is more to this guy than his "black magic" that he was using on him.

Once inside the house, A.J. could not resist the temptation to pull Emmitt close to him and kiss him on the cheek. Emmitt's response was a bit surprising. He put his hands on A.J. 's shoulders and said, "slow down," we have all night. Let's get to know each other before we crawl in bed. I am into passion not just sex.

They sat for some time in the richly appointed den of the house where they found out that they were both the same age of 28 and were at the opposite ends of the income bracket. Emmitt said that his Tonga home was his vacation get-away and that he lived in a non-conspicuous bungalow in Tahiti where he conducted his business affairs. He left A.J. to only imagine what business he was in. A.J. told Emmitt that he worked as a CPA for a small firm in Fiji and takes a trip to Tonga every so many months with his mates for R&R (rest & relaxation) a couple times a year. This is only the second time he has been here, that is why he is so anxious to be with him and have some fun.

Both of them were smart enough to know that each lied. A.J.'s body language was sending nervous vibes all over the place. Emmitt just set there looking into his deep brown eyes and his sexual body as A.J. spread his legs apart, unknowingly revealing his enormous manhood outlined in his white jeans. A.J. inquired, do you have a pardner? The answer was no. Emmitt said, in my business they only get in the way. I don't mix business with pleasure. How would you like a tour of my humble abode? Without thinking A.J. replied, sounds inviting to me.

Emmitt led the way through a maze of doors and floors until they reached the top deck of the house, peering 4 stories above the street below. That deck had a small swimming pool, lounge chairs, a bedroom in one corner with a bath attached, and a full bar. It was covered with thick green Astroturf which made it look like a garden paradise. A.J. thought to himself that his business in Tahiti must be very lucrative because no expense has been spared on this home just to be a get-away location.

As they were sitting there waiting for the next move, Emmitt said, apparently you want something from me, what is it? A.J. was put on the spot. Now is the time for a bit of honesty. Nothing to lose but his virginity, he said, I want to have sex with a man for the first time. I want to say turn over a new leaf in my life and explore a new lifestyle. Emmitt said, why would you want to do that? People just don't turn gay, they are born that way, what's your excuse? He replied, all of my life I have had this deep fantasy of having a male lover, but local customs and religion forbid such relationships. I am miles away from home now and this time, while I am on R&R, I want to explore my fantasy to see if it is for me or not.

Emmitt got up from his chair next to the pool and started to take off his clothes piece by piece. His shaved head and Black skin were hairless except around his spear that hung limp between his legs. He looked like an Aborigine Warrior ready for battle. He was so strikingly handsome as he dove into the pool. A.J. stripped off all his clothing and joined him in the water, without noticing his erection, that was growing larger and larger with each passing second. When they were both in the water, A.J. swam up to Emmitt and put his arms and legs around him as an indication for him to take his virginity.

After the brief encounter underwater, Emmitt put his arm around A.J. 's neck and led him to the king-size bed where he threw him down face first. He then continued where he had left off in the pool. A.J. never thought that such pleasure could be enjoyed in this passionate way especially with another man. It far exceeds the enjoyment that he once had with his wife/girlfriend in NZ. Emmitt then rolled A.J. over on his back and kissed him so passionately A.J. climaxed all over himself. A.J. never experiencing such passion, also never experienced climaxing all over himself twice, before. Emmitt, rolled over completely exhausted of all his "black magic" that he used with passion, on A.J.

When A.J. returned to the Ghost Ship his white jeans were riding low on his thin brown waist and he had his shirt thrown over his right shoulder. His man 's scent was of raw natural odor of sex. He went down two flights of stairs and was walking toward his stateroom, when on the starboard side a door opened. It was Jamison, very black, 6'3" tall gorgeous man. He towered over A.J. like the Statue of Liberty.

They both stopped and stared into each other's eyes. Didn't know you were our neighbor, said Jamison. A.J. said, if I were not so tired and fucked out, I would be through that doorway in an instance and find out who else is in there with you. Be at lunch tomorrow, then you will find out, Jamison said.

Jamison shared the chance encounter with Stephen, his pardner for many years. They both started as crew on a smaller TITO, then became skilled as "Executive-Service' cartel members. Since then, their life together has been more than either could expect living in the world of the cartel. They both agreed the King runs the most unique gay cartel, and in **Lucifer's** opinion, in the heavens and hell, none compare.

Jamison had saved Stephen's life during the birthday party that was planned for King 3 years ago on a remote island north of Tonga.

When armed mercenaries boarded the TITO II and a bloody hand to hand battle took place, Stephen was hurt badly from a machete waving cartel member that Jamison executed, with precision, during the bloodbath. Simon, head of security, patched Stephen up and he recovered completely, leaving only a scar on his left shoulder. Lucky for Stephen, the slight scar only added to his muscled 6' lightly suntanned brown body, that Jamison could not resist.

The headquarters yacht, the TITO V, carried the 3 leaders of the Ghost Cartel; a crew of 8, and only 4 teams (8) cartel members, for the King & David's protection. Simon, head of security, had never stopped investigating the leak that set the birthday party massacre into motion. He discovered that some of the cartels came as far away as a remote island off NZ.

The entire staff and crew were sitting on the top deck of the Ghost Ship enjoying the view of the harbor when their new guest arrived for lunch. He looked rather tired but freshly showered and apparently had borrowed some clothes from the storage locker because he had on black pants that hung from the waist and a T-shirt equally as large. A.J. greeted everyone with an informal greeting and took a seat next to Jamison and his pardner Stephen. He told Stephen it was a pleasure to meet him and that he had met his partner in the hallway last night. Stephen acknowledged the event and continued eating.

Simon, with his uncanny ability to detect trouble before trouble starts, asked A.J. the name of the cartel he was associated with in NZ. A.J. was not as worldly as Simon or King in the world of cartels. He simply replied, "The Killer Beez." Simon thought to himself, during the execution of some of the captives they revealed that they were ordered to the island by "The Killer Beez" from NZ. Bells and whistles went off in Simon's head and he instantly got up and went to the man cave on the second level of the yacht. He placed a call to GYS security to get a run down on "who's who" in "The Killer Beez Cartel." He was nervously waiting for the reply when Winston walked in. He asked Simon what was going on. That he looked worked up.

Simon just sat there and shook his head and said, "I can't believe it."

Simon said, the Ghost Ship has traveled thousands of miles in the waters of the South Pacific without detection and now, I think we have on board a cartel member that played a role in the loss of life and damage to the vessels of the Ghost Cartel. Winston sat down and said, "it must be the new face onboard". "You're right about that," Simon said. Winston went on to say, call King and David, we need to meet right away.

The four of them met in the office on the top deck of the Ghost Ship. Detailed plans were put in motion to gain information from A.J. on his knowledge and/

or involvement in the massacre. They noticed when he showed up for lunch that he was carrying on a conversation with Jamison and Stephen. King called them to the man cave to find out what the conversation was all about. Jamison explained the close encounter that he had with A.J. the night before. It sounded like he had been manhandled before returning to the yacht that night and he was too tired, and his comment, to join Stephen and I in our quarters.

Simon informed both of them that he was a member of a cartel called "The Killer Beez" from NZ. That cartel combined with others planned and executed the attack on King's birthday party three years ago on July 6th. What we need to know is how involved he was in this mess. His involvement will determine his fate. Jamison replied, "I think we can manage that."

After lunch Jameson asked the foreman of Tonga Headquarters if he could borrow one of his "go-boats" to take a ride around some of the beautiful uninhabited islands in the Kingdom of Tonga. Permission granted, he went to their suite and shared the information that he received from Simon with his pardner Stephen. Then they began planning their next move. Simon placed King and David's life in their hands, what an honor, this mission cannot fail.

All three of them, dressed only in skimpy swim attire, boarded a 50' "go-boat" and headed out of the harbor due North to a chain of islands so beautiful that a person could not resist exploring. The West side of the islands that had white sandy beaches, the opposite side had black sand with the hidden danger of saltwater crocodiles. With Jamison at the wheel, he guided the boat around several of the islands to check out the concealed threats. Once he knew the perfect landing area for the boat, he headed it in at half throttle, to safely beach the craft. They all jumped out to enjoy the perfect white sandy beach paradise.

Once on the sand, Jamison and Stephen threw their swimsuits in the boat and rolled in the sand like two little boys meeting for the first time. Stephen's 6' suntanned chocolate body with close cropped wavy hair and a man size spear equal to his lover Jamison was a sight that excited A.J. to the core. He instantly got an erection that could be seen islands away. His erection was so long, and smooth Jamison and Stephen were envious. How could his little guy be so well endowed, they thought? Then they thought about their mission.

Jamison, the more aggressive of the two pardners, asked A.J. What does he do with all that meat between his legs? The reply was, "I am trying all things new since turning over a new lifestyle." What do you mean "new lifestyle" Jamison inquired? A.J. replied, when I was with my former cartel, I lived with a woman that I referred to as my wife. In that cartel, gay sex was taboo, and gays were often times executed on the spot if they showed any sign of weakness. Jamison said, "What were your primary duties for the cartel? His reply was, "accounting, planning hist, movement of money, payroll, and almost everything that David does for your organization. I was one of a handful of confidants of the leader of the Beez.

Jamison and Stephen both took A.J. by both arms and pushed him down on the white sand and held his arms over his head. They spread eagle his legs and firmly grabbed his nuts which only intensified the hardness of his erection. Then asked him, "how about hits on other cartels, did you plan or have any part in the execution of those hits"?

No, was his reply. That was above my paygrade. Those plans come from the very top of the Beez command structure, and they are scattered all over the islands.

Stephen said, how would you like to taste the juice of real cartel men who fight to the death for their lovers? Remembering the techniques from Emmitt the night before, he started licking each of them all over, not missing a spot. As their juices flowed, he drank them up as if a Hennessy without the rocks. A.J. said this is an entirely new lifestyle for me, it takes some getting used to. Stephen said, it feels like you are adjusting without too much hesitation. They spent several hours sunbathing on the beach. When all three felt the sun's burn on their skin, they boarded their boat and headed back to Tonga. Mission accomplished, they thought. The chance encounter had proven to King that they were skilled in their profession and be trusted to protect the cartel.

The two week visit at Tonga headquarters ended when the TITO V pulled out of the harbor heading due west for the island of Fiji, the 450 mile trip to visit Jamal & Lankenua's operation was long overdue. They had set up a small but profitable operation in the port city of Suva, its capital. It lay at the mouth of the Rewa River and the Sava Harbor which were regular stops for transpacific shipping. J&L could not have picked a sweeter spot to establish their operation as every drug shipment east or west came through that port.

To date, their $15 million in profits, during the last four months, have made them one of the top producers for the cartel. Capt. Oliver voyage to Fiji that would pass some of the most scenic uninhabited islands in the South Pacific. Chef Jeffrey had stock the pantry with fine food for the voyage, so King, Winston, and David were just relaxing in the man cave taking in the eye sparkling sights of the many islands they passed at a distance.

As night approached David was in his suite on the same deck as King and Winston. There was a knock on his door. When he answered it, there stood A.J. in black short shorts. That manly bulge of his was curled up so big that the top three buttons wouldn't close. David said, "what do you need", with a blank smile on his face. I thought that I could spend some time with you to get to know you. You spend most of your time with King and I don't notice you interacting with the rest of the crew that much.

David, still standing in the doorway, replied, "I told you, "I am the only remaining member of the original Marquis Cartel. As such King and I have the responsibility for every member of this cartel and its profitability. I don't have time to waste on insufficient relationships.

King protects me from all of that and has since Jim, my original love, died several years ago. May I come in, A.J. asked? Still bewildered, David said, only for a bit, I have work to do before we arrive in Fiji.

When A.J. entered his suite, he was amazed, it was as big and plush as King's. Far too grand and big for one individual. He asked David what he does with all the room. David responded, "not much, I work here and sleep here, that's about it. I often take meals in my room as this is my sanctuary from the cartel world. My former love and I had been together for years and came from the world of banking. The safe and secure world is just opposite of where I am today. I use all of my financial training to benefit our cartel. King makes sure that no harm comes my way. Have you slept with King, A.J. asked. "I am not gay," replied David. I have a platonic relationship with him that is stronger than any bond. I suggest you respect that, never cross King, as it will be the last thing you ever do.

A.J. was sitting on the sofa looking around the massive suite and he saw a picture on the nightstand next to David's bed. He inquired as to who was in the picture? David replied that was taken on Marquis Island with Jim and I, at Jim's final party before he succumbed to cancer. A.J. replied, Jim was a very handsome man. David said, "The love of my life, it has been most difficult living without him. He had a special charm about him that dazzled people." After he lost his lover Ron, he and King became lovers. Jim was King's first love.

What an amazing couple they made. **Beauty and the Beast** let's say.

So, you have never had a sexual pardner, is that correct? That's right, I have not found it necessary to swing either way. How do you relieve your sexual urges? David replied, over the years I have learned to manage that too. The choice I have is King and an abundance of security and unconditional love or an unknown person and my security thrown to the wind. I have made the right decision for myself. A.J. sat mystified on the sofa wondering how such an attractive individual could resist all temptations in life to bond with King, the leader of the notorious Jamaican cutthroat cartel. David said, I am planning to do it. I suggest you leave me to it. I don't appreciate unexpected visitors to my suite, so I suggest you go. A.J. got up and walked toward the door, gave David a kiss on the cheek and departed toward his stateroom.

The next day around noon the Ghost Ship was 25 miles outside the capital city of Suva when Capt. Oliver placed a call to Jamal at their Fiji location, He requested docking instruction, as this was the first time that King and the TITO V had visited their new location. Jamal instructed Oliver to idle in place for a brief period until he could locate a mooring at the Royal Suva Yacht Club that would accommodate the 250' vessel.

In about a half an hour Jamal contacted Capt. Oliver to inform him that a shore boat would meet them within 5 minutes to guide them past the many shipwrecks dotting the yacht club's entrance and that he had secured two cement mooring for them while in port. He and Lankenua will be waiting for them upon arrival. Just a reminder, he registered the yacht under its registration numbers instead of the name for their safety, as the TITO V is the Ghost Ship.

King was standing on the outer railing of the vessel as it was being secured to the moorings. When completed, he told Jamal & Lankenua to join him in the man cave of the yacht. When they entered the door, King had forgotten how exquisitely handsome they were. To love them, enjoy them, all will be lost, was their calling card. Let's have a drink, King said. He went on to say, you two have really made us some money since coming to Fiji.

Jamal replied, it didn't come without some sacrifice. The first hit we made on Waya Island; we underestimated the crew of the freighter carrying the shipment and two of my men were shot but recovered. We did retrieve the load but too much blood was lost for the small amount of money we made. We got permission from David to purchase two more "go-boats" to add to our arsenal, bringing the total to 4 so that we could carry out the entire cartel crew for a hit. Since then we have not had any major problems to deal with.

David asked how far is your operation center from here? Lankenua replied, ten miles. By "go-boat" 5 minutes up the Rewa River. It is the longest and widest river in Fiji, making it a perfect place to hide. Chef Jeffery is preparing a late lunch, so join us and we can catch up on all the news around the Ghost Cartel and I am sure all on board will be happy to see you, David said. Just then the "Black Falcon" walked in and gave King a kiss on the cheek. J & L were taken back by King's sign of affection that he displayed so casually. What had happened to him, they wondered. Since Jim's passing over 3 years ago, King has been a cold stone killer who has given orders without mercy, only protecting David.

Chef Jeffery served "Lenner" or late lunch on the aft deck of the Ghost Ship. That was the same deck where the swimming pool had been covered with teak flooring to make a large setting area. On the long sidebar an array of food was laid out that looked like a picture postcard. J & L were surrounded by their fellow cartel members catching up on current events when a stranger walked up from the lower deck clad only in tight black short shorts. It seemed as if all eyes were glued on him as he helped himself to the assortment of food. He sat down next to Kenny, who he had not met yet. Kenny said it would be a good idea if you go below and grab a shirt. King doesn't like flaunting our souls at the table unless it is our original tribunal attire.

A.J. returned wearing a low-cut black tank top.

When he entered the room for the second time Jamal looked at him quite concerned. He said to his pardner Lankenua, haven't we seen that guy someplace before? Yes, I believe we did. I don't remember where, but it wasn't between the sheets. I'll remember, give me some time. They all continued their small talk around the table while the afternoon sun began to set on the western horizon. Chef Jeffery said that he and Tommy would be serving a late dinner at 8 p.m. for those who were still hungry.

King told J & L that they could stay on the TITO V for the night and first thing, after breakfast, they would take two "go-boats" to review their operation on the Rewa River. Jamal asked why two? King said, "I learned a long time ago not to group the leaders of the cartel together in one spot, for safety protocol. I want to take several of my personal bodyguards with me, so two boats provide that ability, then a 5 minute boat ride should be a non-eventful. Jamal said, King, you are always thinking ahead of any potential problems.

The next day after breakfast Winston asked if there were any volunteers that would like to take a ride to J & L's operation center and 5-minute boat ride away. We need 4 cartel members and our personal bodyguards. Without hesitation A.J. raised both hands to make sure he got Winston's attention. He took note of all the names and went to the office to inform King of the list of 8 volunteers. King read off the names to the group and David spoke up. Last night A.J. stopped by my suite seemingly doing research on what I do and who I sleep with. I told him to leave so that I don't have time to waste and small talk and he kissed me on the cheek before he left, which I found alarming. King was enraged by that comment.

Lankenua spoke up, I remember where I saw him. Jamal you should remember, we were in the Colonel Bar, the exclusive retreat known as a drug dealer social spot in Suva. He was with 3 or 4 other guys. They were all drunk and throwing money around like it was water. He was sitting on one guy's lap kissing him and the others were with women. What in the fuck is going on here, King asked? King called Simon to the office. He explained the entire situation to Simon. Told him to investigate the situation and get back to him immediately.

King chose 4 cartel members and his personal bodyguards and departed for the J & L operation center soon after breakfast leaving A.J. on the yacht. It was a quick stay. Their profits speak for themselves, they were using low flying watercraft to transport their heist to Tonga for redistribution. All aspects of their operation were well greased, and their crew polished to integrate into the islands of Fiji. King said, "I think it is time we went out to sea. There is work to be cleaned up on our end."

TREASON

*A*s mentioned before there is nothing worse a cartel member can do is to turn on one's own cartel, it's a death sentence. Treason to your cartel is death without mercy. It took several days while the Ghost Ship was slowly cruising toward Tonga, in the open waters of the South Pacific, when Simon came into the office where King, Winston, and David were busy analyzing the next location that they wanted to visit. King looked up to recognize Simon's presence and said, "what news do you have for us? Not good, I am sorry to say." Why are you sorry, King replied? We don't deal with sorry's.

A.J. is a fucked up lying cheat. Apparently, he has pulled off this shit with several smaller cartels working his way up to us. All of the cartels he has been associated with have vanished out of the South Pacific. I can't put a finger on the cartel he works for. It seems he is a freelancer. He works for the highest bidder. His story changes from job to job. Apparently, he is paid a large sum of money to gain information on each cartel he infiltrates. Information for hire is a game. He is not a killer but the cartels that employ him are ruthless. Now what, Simon said? King said, thank you Simon, we will take it from here. King looked at Winston and David and said we had a problem on our hands that I should have detected from the very start. No one turns on their cartel, which is treason. We can play his game just as well as he can. Let's catch the rat in his own trap.

Turning on a cartel is so dangerous a person cannot even imagine anyone doing it. A.J. must have the feeling that he is so undetectable that he just doesn't use common sense in his actions. Apparently allowing his sexual emotions to get in the way of the well-founded knowledge of life in a cartel. King asked David if he would play the rat to catch A.J. in his own tracks before he got the information he needed on the Ghost, David replied, of course, just let me know what you think I should do. King said. I told Capt. Olive, which reduce our speed to 5 knots, which will extend our trip to Tonga by two days. That will give you time to invite him to your suite and continue the informal discussion that he wanted on his first visit, but this time act a bit more friendly. David said, I can act friendly but nothing more than that. If things get out of my control, I will call you to rescue me, if he makes sexual advances. "That's a deal," said King. Keep your intercom line open while he is in your room so that we can hear everything he says that way I can be there in a flash. Ok, David said. Let's put the plan into action.

By late afternoon, the crew of the Ghost Ship had untied it from the cement moorings and were now heading due southeast toward The Kingdom of Tonga. That night David made it a point to acknowledge A.J. with a warm smile at dinner. A.J. was flatter with the flirtation. Later that night there was a knock-on David's door. He instantly knew who it was. Before he opened the door, he switched his intercom on and verified with King that it was transmitting. When he opened the door there stood A.J. clad only in a towel as if just getting out of the shower. David acted surprised to see him, even though he wasn't. He said, what up A.J.? Just thought I would drop by for a quick visit before bedtime, was his reply. Early to bed, early to rise, makes a man healthy, wealthy, and wise," A.J. said.

David said, "I am very wealthy, quite healthy, and wiser than most, so what are you after that I need that King doesn't provide me with"?

A.J.'s quick reply was, "a good fuck. How do you like it, are you top or bottom" he asked. David was so taken back by his direct approach but invited him in to set the trap just as King had planned. David said, "Want a drink"? I don't have much to offer. Just sodas and juices. I don't come here for a drink other than that of man juice. David had to use his imagination to decipher that reply. He said, just have a seat on the sofa, I have some free time, I am caught up with all of my work, A.J. sat down on the large sofa across from David's chair and flung open his towel. OMG David thought he was hung bigger and more beautiful than King and Winston combined, no wonder he poses such a threat to everyone he meets.

David said, I suggest you close your towel. I told you before that I am loved and in love with King who protects me. Where is he now to protect you from this big beautiful manly tool that could penetrate an elephant and make it moan for more." David then took bull by the horns and said, what is it that you want from me other than a good fuck? A.J. said, just to get to the point after a good roll in the hay, where are all of your operation centers located in the South Pacific?

With A,J,'s towel flung open, David walked out of his suite and immediately King walked in. So you

would like to know where all of our operations centers are? Well A.J., leave that towel off, I would like to
show you off to the crew before you see a map of our
locations.

David's suite was on the first level below deck. King
guided A.J., naked around and through all the decks of
the Ghost Ship ending up in the man cave just below
the office. Over the intercom King announced that a
crew meeting will be held on the aft deck in 5 minutes,
where he would put A.J, on full display for all to, let's
say, not to enjoy, but to witness, as he would soon have
his elephant sized dick trimmed to a size that would not
inflict pain on anything bigger than a rat, which he was.

A.J. was strutting around in all of his glory, thinking that his dick was the biggest on the yacht. All the
cartel members did not have any idea what was going
to happen. King asked each one of them to take a feel
of that elephant hanging between his legs and as they
did it became totally erect. A.J. felt like the master of
the vessel. Then King dismissed the cartel and took
A.J. to the bottom deck of the Ghost Ship. When he
opened the door there was the operating room and
surgical table. A.J. asked what was going on? King said,
I think it was time we got some insightful information
from you." What is it you want to know? A.J. said.

With A.J. strapped to the surgical table and his legs secured in its stirrups. Winston brought out the scalpel; sweat drops appeared on A.J.'s brow. Winston stood over A.J. and asked, how many cartels have you infiltrated? How much have you made from the information that you collected on them? How much of the information that you have you shared with us is true? A.J. quickly responded. Okay everyone, you caught me, let's say with my pants down. Here's the facts and nothing but the facts. Four cartels. A total of $5,000.00 in cash which I have hidden away. I like to bottom, even with the size of my dick, my greatest pleasure is getting it put to me. I am a rat and I know that is a death sentence within any cartel. So, let's get on with it. My time is up, just make it quick and clean.

I don't think so, King said. A cartel rat's execution is never quick and clean, you are begging for the limited life you have left. A.J. said then do what you want, I know you will anyway. King took his elephant size dick in his hands, which has now shrunk to a manageable size, his balls weren't hanging low any longer. His public hair had grown out considerably which made everything between his legs look more manly. King said, "Winston, take a look at this." They both stood there over the surgical table in awe of the natural beauty of this cartel rat and shook their heads. King asked David, "What do you want to do with all of this natural beauty"? David replied, he is the most beautiful man I have ever seen, present company excluded, Let's not kill him, David said, you are getting soft my dear friend. Do you want to keep him for yourself? David replied, give me a little time to think about that.

DAVID & A.J.

*D*avid loosened the straps around A.J.'s arms and legs and led him to his suite two decks up. He said we are a day out of Tonga and your life is still in King's hands, but King won't do anything to you without asking me first. You are so extremely handsome, why would you put your life in danger for a measly $5,000? A.J., we have billions. All of us on board are the finest "Executive-Service" cartel members in our specialized profession. I have so much money, but money doesn't buy love, I found that out a long time ago when I lost Jim, my first love.

A.J. said, we came from the opposite side of the tracks. You were taken care of by Jim for years. I was born poor and lived hand to mouth for years until I educated myself by working on the streets and then hustling the rich guys to make a dollar. Thank God I had the equipment to get the job done. I have never had a meaningful relationship that I can trust or be trusted. You are the first person that showed any concern for my personal wellbeing.

David sat there quietly and spoke. What do we do now? A.J. said, "What do you think we should do"? That is an extremely complicated question David said, why don't you spend the night with me, because I know you will be safe here and I will talk to King in the morning. Did you want a drink? A.J. said that would be great, I really need one. David called the Steward, and he showed up to take drink orders. A.J. had his usual Hennessy on the rocks but this time a triple. David had a diet coke. When they finished their drinks A.J. was as loose as a goose in heat as David watched him wander off to the shower to wash off the sweat from the fate he had just experienced in the surgical unit.

David went to bed. Rolled over watching A.J. walking nude out of the bathroom. What a beautiful sight, he got a sexual tingle all over his body. That had only happened once when he, Ron, and Jim had spent a night together, but their personal boundaries never crossed. He really didn't know how he was going to react to this manly god. He got out of bed and went to King's room. David told King, "I am really fond of A.J. There is something nice about him that is undiscovered. He is soft and gentle. Let's give him a chance to prove his worth. King replied, if you say so David. It's your cartel too. We just won't give him too much rope, we don't want him to hang himself so soon. He might take a little training in our way of life on the Ghost Ship. David said great and returned to his suite with an anxious smile on his face.

When he got back, A.J. with a sleepy voice said, "where have you been? David said, had to take care of a little business. David pulled back the black silk sheets and slid into bed. At that very moment A.J. pulled up next to him, put his arms around him and fell asleep. All night David was awakened by the sound of A.J. purring like a little kitty. Oftentimes he would roll-over and smell him to remind himself just how special A.J. was, even though A.J. did not realize it yet. When morning arrived David departed his suite, as he did, he looked back at A.J. who was still asleep. His sweet man scent from the shower the night before was still lingering in the air.

He joined King and Winston in the man cave for breakfast. The first words out of King's mouth were "how was your night." David just looked at him with an inquisitive eye and said nothing. David then said, "I don't think it is necessary to return to headquarters, we are all fueled, and our pantries are full, we can stay at sea for a month without docking. Let's enjoy a cruise around some of the smaller islands of our playground giving all on board a chance to get to know A.J. and he a chance to settle into his new environment. Just like you said, "give him enough rope to hang himself if he so chooses". King replied, go tell Capt. Oliver the plan David.

After breakfast David went up to the bridge. He instructed Capt. Oliver to charter an easy course around and through the uninhabited islands in the Oceanic Chain. Oliver was mystified as to the quick change of plans but followed David's orders and headed North away from Tonga, their original destination. Not long after the course was changed, King called for a crew meeting on the aft deck and informed everyone that they were taking a little rest break for a few days, and to kick back and enjoy themselves.

When David returned to his suite A.J. was still asleep. He went over a nudged his shoulder. When he did A.J. came up fighting, but soon realized that it was David and that he was tucked away in a beautiful luxury suite on the TITO V. Sorry about that reaction David, A.J. commented, then got out of bed complete-ly naked and went to the bathroom. David watched every step he took as he walked across the suite and disappeared behind a wall blocking his view of the elephant man. David walked into the bath and said, "do you mind if I shower while you finish up"? A.J. smiled and said, "please do." David slowly moved all of his clothing, piece by piece, like a strip show in a gay bar, A.J. sat on the bathroom counter and enjoyed the beauty of David's smooth body covered with fine blond hair. His chest hair ran all the way down to his naval, then his bush was so thick his manhood was barely detectable. When David stepped out of the shower A.J. was there to meet him with a big white towel. Let me do the honors, he dried David from head to toe, rubbing his manhood fondly and soon it became an extension of joy and happiness combined. David just stood there not knowing exactly what to do, so he just let A.J. take the lead.

When A.J. was finished he gave David a kiss on the cheek and said we better get dress and go topside or else everyone on board will think we have been fucking. David was surprised that A.J. had passed up the opportunity to jump his boner, he asked himself, why? After they both got dressed David escorted A.J. to the galley where there was always food to eat 24/7. A.J. was still overwhelmed by the vastness of the Ghost Ship. Not only was it pristine but immense. He could easily get lost within its many floors and compartments. David said, we are not going back to Tonga, instead I have instructed the captain to stay at sea for a few days so the entire crew can have a well-deserved rest. What a great idea, A.J. said.

David, feeling more in-charge than in the past, came right out and asked A.J. "what information have you passed on to other cartels about the ghost"? At this very moment in time **nothing**. I was so captivated by you and King, I wanted to be part of you or your cartel. I would be honored to be your mate. A cartel member I am not trained for, remember I am a CPA and like yourself outstanding at the financial end of the business. David said, that is a long wish for a condemned man. I think it would be easier to be a member of a cartel than my mate, as I have never had one and I don't know if I want one, as you picture it. Maybe we can start off slow, like I did with Jim. A platonic relationship and see if we jell, then take it day by day. If it doesn't work for any reason, nothing will be lost except a friendship, A.J. agreed.

King and the "Black Falcon" were kicked back in the man cave enjoying each other's company. Staring out of the 360 degree windows at the blue South Pacific

Ocean. King called Oliver and instructed him to keep a close eye on the radar for any approaching watercraft, because no matter what A.J. had told David about his involvement with information leaked on the ghost, he was not taking any chances. Capt. Oliver said that he had already set their automatic radar warning system at 75 miles and he would sound the alarm if there were any approaching craft by sea or air. King and Winston retired to their suite next to David's on the lower deck and crawled in the shower together to wash each other's masculine bodies before they engaged in such manly sex that the vessel seemed to roll with the motion of their pleasure. Laying sexually exhausted on their king size bed King & Winston, just talked for a long while about what the future could look like if once again, they slowly retired from the drug business and focused on their personal safety.

King reached over Winston's chest and grabbed the intercom summoning David to their cabin. When David received the call he excused himself from A.J. and immediately went to King's suite next door. He opened the door and walked in and King and Winston were laying there naked as a J-Bird on the king size bed. King asked David how much money they had, and how much they had coming in monthly from their worldwide operation. David thought for a minute and said too much. I can't give you the exact amount, but it is in the billions. It is stashed away in accounts all over the world and on board the TITO V itself how much do we have King? Billions was his reply.

The mansion on Marquis Island is still loaded with money in its underground vaults. So, what are we talking about here, David replied. King said, the last time you spoke to us about all of our exorbitant wealth you suggested we take a break and retire from the cartel business and enjoy the fruits of our labor. How about we do that again? King asked David. David was completely in shock by King's statement. That is more than a good idea, David said. What prompted you to make that decision King? I am in love again and I want to enjoy Winston and you as long as time allows. How about we head for the Hawaiian Islands. Do you want me to tell Capt. Oliver to charter a course? Yes, King replied, and made it a slow one.

HAWAIIAN ISLANDS

*D*avid walked up to Captains bridge and instructed Oliver to chart a course for the Hawaiian Islands. During the conversation he inquired as to the miles. Oliver charted it out at 3100 miles and with the fuel capacity of the yacht at a maximum range of four thousand miles the islands are well within range. David instructed Capt. Oliver to notify all crew members of our planned 12-day voyage so that they can ready the Ghost Ship for the extended time at sea.

David called King to the office on the top deck and reminded him that the Hawaiian Islands were within the limits of the United States. Once again DEA, FBI, and the rest of the law enforcement agencies will be looking for anyone connected to drugs or money laundering. King asked David if he had set up any accounts in the islands and he said no, but I could transfer in a small amount, like under $10,000 without any red flags. Then keep feeding the account with small transfers periodically not to draw suspicion on us. King said, $10,000 doesn't even fill the yacht with fuel. David replied, then we need to stop along the way to refuel and stock up on supplies before we hit American soil. That is a good idea, King said. Tell Oliver to make it happen.

Northern Soma was identified as the stop to refuel and resupply the Ghost Ship, as Southern Soma is a province of the USA. The 320-mile voyage was charted to avoid any encounter with hostel islands enroute. When they arrived in Port Apia the cement dock was more than adequate to accommodate the 250' TITO V. Their Somalia operation headed up by Mbinga & Kathai revenue was consistent month after month. They placed a phone call to them requesting their presence for a late dinner on the Ghost Ship while the crew visited the sights of the small town.

Wayne had been reading "Treasure Island '' during his days at sea and when he and Oliver were roaming the streets they noticed a sign, "birthplace of Robert Louis Stevenson" the Scottish novelist and the author of Wayne's unfinished novel. Wayne said, Oliver, let's check this place out. When they got there they discovered Stevenson had lived there the last years of his life and his home is now the official residence of the Head of State of Northern Soma. Being rather grand, they thought, RLS stories and poems were known around the world, which provided him with the luxury of a comfortable lifestyle. Now finishing Treasure Island is next on his bucket list.

Dinner with their Somalian leaders was uneventful. Their operation was well organized and profitable. Both of them shared stories from home. Kaikai from Tanzania and Mbinga from Kenya both fishermen who enjoyed their off time fishing the blue waters surrounding their island paradise. They also informed David that they had not been hassled by any USA authorities concerning monies deposited or transferred of any size because North Soma is not part of the Federal Reserve reporting system.

Before the Ghost Ship departed, David went to the bank and opened two accounts under the name of their LLC with sizable deposits of cash. Then all fueled and resupplied for its voyage to Hawaii, the TITO V pulled out of the Port of Apia heading North once again for a leisurely cruise to the island paradise that Americans called Hawaii.

Capt. Oliver and Wayne studied the charter of the 132 Hawaiian Islands. Only 7 of them were inhabited.

They noticed that two were uninhabited. Niihau and Kahoolawe. Molokai belonged to Singapore based **GL-LTD.** And the other two were forbidden islands. The island of Molokai was once known as the **leper colony of Kalaupapa**, from 1865 to 1969 prior to being leased by GL-LTD. Niihau has been privately owned by the Sinclair/Robinson family since 1864 and travel to the island was by invitation only.

125 uninhabited islands, how great, we can get lost for weeks in this so-called paradise, Capt. Oliver said. Oliver called King on the intercom and informed him of the information about the islands. King said, stay clear of all USA ports. We want to lay low for a while, it's R&R time for all on board. The Ghost Ship, as it is called, cruised silently amongst the small island, anchoring offshore in their coral reef harbors during the day and slipping on to a new location during the night.

David and A.J. spent time together talking in detail about their childhoods and upbring. David was raised by a devout Christian family with the highest of moral values. He was educated at the University of San Francisco and hired by Jim, his first love, to work as his assistant at the bank in the same city. They spent five years at the bank together before getting into the import/export business that belonged to Jim's former lover **Tito**, who was killed in Vietnam. That is why all of their yachts are named after him, as a tribute to his first love of his life.

A.J. story was not as pleasant. Born to a single Mother who was addicted to drugs. Sold her body to make the cash for drugs, and he learned at an early age to sell his body to gain favors of any kind to gain any small pleasure in life. Even his simple clothing had to be purchased with cash from selling his small elephant to willing buyers. His elephant was always larger than normal for those his own age but he didn't realize it until he was about 15 years old when he met another guy his age who was very wealthy. That guy paid handsomely for an all-nighter. They young man could not take what A.J. had to real out, so A.J. rolled over and took him with ease. All of A.J.'s life up to and including every day until he came aboard the TITO V was like that. SEX, SEX, and more SEX for hire. I dreaded face every morning, he said. Now I can sleep in, I don't care about sex, I have had enough. Passion, I want more than anything now. If sex happens, that would be great too.

David laid back on the black silk sheets and rolled over on his side and looked at A.J. laying there so beautifully innocent. He said, A.J. why can't it be like this all of the time? A.J. replied because life's complicated with rules. In the morning David slipped out of bed quietly and took a quick shower. Dressed in white shorts and tank top with deck shoes, no socks of course, and was heading out the door. He looked back at A.J. laying there now naked on the silk sheets, as chocolate as a Milky Way candy bar, curled up in the natal position. His body is as smooth as ice from the neck down. The bottoms of his feet were so white, David thought it must have been from years of walking barefoot through the slums of NZ where he grew up. David left the room and headed to the office via the galley to grab a cup of java.

While the Ghost Ship was anchored in a crystal blue lagoon of a small coral reef island for a few days, David decided he would review the monthly financial reports. As he always did, he just looked at the bottom line first. The variance was too great not to further analyze net income, unit by unit. When he did, he noted that New Zealand's income had dropped from its norm of $8 million down to $0 for the last reporting period. David reported his findings to King who was surprised as New Zealand was managed by Ian & Cyprian who they had just visited over a month ago. King put a call into their operation center and Ian answered. King inquired, what is going on down there, your profits are in the tank? Ian said, I know. Our leads from our cartel source have dried up and shipment into NZ has been diverted to unknown ports. We have not been able to get our hands on the information yet. We are running in the red right now. We need a big hit to bail us out. Who was your source once again? A.J, Ian replied.

David said, A.J. told me that he fed shipment information to them for his escape out of NZ, don't you remember? Winston said, let's call him up here right away to get the lowdown. When A.J. arrived at the office David informed him of the large variance they discovered in their monthly report from NZ. It was over $8 million short, and Ian confirmed that he had been the source for most if not all of the leads. A.J. said, that is correct, my million-dollar ticket out of NZ before I was detected as a snitch.

Ian just told us that the shipments have been diverted to other locations and they have not been able to find them. A.J. replied, they are looking in the wrong parts of the islands. They probably are running them through the area outside their Territorial Authority. NZ has over 600 islands and many of them can be used as transfer points for drug shipments. There is such a high demand for drugs in the North and South NZ mainland, so shipments, I am sure are still flowing in, they have to be.

King called Ian and put the call on the speakerphone in the office. When Ian answered King informed him that A.J, David, and Winston were listening and talking with his former connection to get an update on drug shipments. Ian said, "How are you doing A.J.," Ian asked. Never happier, A.J. replied, he went on to say, "I hear you are having a problem locating shipments? Ian said, since you disappeared off the face of the earth, so did the shipments. A.J. just laughed. The dealers know what I knew, so they avoided those islands and ports.

Remember that party where you met me in Christchurch at the bigtime drug dealer's mansion? That's where you can get all the current information you need. That guy I had to service several times and I mean several times to make you that $8 million and my ticket to freedom. There is no way I can return there, because if I did I would be killed before I could make a phone call. I am more useful to you sitting here safely on the Ghost Ship than in NZ. King said, sounds like you have your work cut out for you and Cyprian, looking forward to seeing the results in your next monthly report.

King thanked A.J. for his assistance. It's a proven fact now that you have put your life at risk twice for us.

Once to make over $8 million and then saved us from that cartel hit as we were passing Wellington in Northern New Zealand. Why is it that you saved us and the other cartels you allowed to be banished from the South Pacific? A.J. said, you should know the answer to that question. The Ghost Cartel and Marquis Cartel are the biggest and best cartels operating in the waters of the South Pacific and Caribbean Sea. Who in their right mind won't want to be a part of it and membership isn't cheap. I risk my life to be where I am today and all I can say is, **"I have never been happier.'** King said why don't you and David take a break from all this paperwork and take the shore boat and explore this beautiful island we are anchored off of. David, take one of my bodyguards along to drive the boat and clear the island just in case there are unknown creatures, either animal or human.

The jet shore boat slowly passed over beautiful coral reefs that looked as if you could touch. Paul, the bodyguard, beached the craft on the white sand and all three jumped out. Paul said stay close to the boat while I take a look around. He grabbed his AR-15 and 45 sidearm and walked into the jungle reappearing down the beach a few feet.

Walking back up the beach toward the two of them he yelled out, hit the sand. Just then his AR-15 rattled off several rounds killing a wild boar that was running full speed toward David from the other end of the beautiful white sand. A.J. said, what a place to get attacked.

Thank you, Paul. His reply was that's my job. David said, and you saved my life, King will be grateful to you for that. Paul instructed them to stay close to the boat and not to wander into the jungle as there were too many unknowns to deal with for one person. Just enjoy the rest of your time on the island and let me know when you're ready to return, I will stand by the bow of the craft, on look out, for the remainder of your stay. After an hour they told Paul that they had enough sun and were ready to return to the Ghost Ship.

When they returned, David told King that Paul had saved their lives from a charging wild boar and thanked him for sending him along.

King then called Paul to the man cave where he had never been before. When Paul arrived he said, gee you have nice digs, we live pretty good, but this is super special I guess one could say, for a very special guy. King just laughed. We are all special on the Ghost. Just want to say thank you personally for taking care of David on the island. You know, I am sure, how very special he is to me. Then King reached into his desk drawer and pulled out a Gold Plated Glock 44 and handed it to him. Oh shit, what a gift, Paul said. King said, let me put it to you this way. If something had happened to David on your watch you would no longer be standing here, so this gift is to recognize the trust I have in you with a person I dearly love.

David and A.J. retired to his suite to freshen up after the sunny day at the beach and to wash off the white sand that was stuck in every crack in their body. Who wants to shower first, A.J. asked. David, with the meekest of voice said, let's shower together. You may wash my back and I will do the same for you. I haven't had my back washed in years. In fact, I can't remember the last time. A.J. said, I am a master at back washes. They both headed to the bathroom where they threw their trunks in the hamper and stood naked in front of each other while the shower was reaching the correct temperature. A.J. 's elephant was growing slowly just looking at David. David put both of his hands on his shoulders and said, "I have never seen a more beautiful man in my life." A..J. looked at David's manhood which was usually buried in all of his blonde pubic hair but now it was totally visible and so delicate.

He was a virgin by rumor and by the looks of it, David's body was inviting him to take what he had never given away before.

They both got into the shower, slowly soaping up each other's bodies. When they got to their backs David put both his hands against the wall of the shower and told A.J. to soap it up very strongly, using a deep massage technique. As A.J. messaged his back David got as hard as he had ever been in his entire life. Since his back was to A.J. he could not see his reaction. As soon as A.J. was finished David said, it was your turn. He turned around quickly, revealing his erection to A.J., who was impressed with the results of the message. He said, it looks like you enjoy your massage? David replied, is it that obvious? Come on David, hard dicks don't lie. Let's see if you enjoy yours. A.J.'s response was the same. His elephant extended so large when he turned around it hit David in the groin sparking an instant sexual attraction between both of them. A.J. once again kissed David on the cheek and they both walked out of the shower and dried each other off. David took his terry cloth robe with the letter "D" off the back of the door and put it on and A.J. wrapped a towel around himself. David said wait a minute, I have a surprise for you. He went out to his room and just delivered a large box with a red bow around it. This is for you. When A.J. opened it, there was a white terry cloth robe with "A.J." embroidered on it. A.J. began to cry. David wiped the tears running down his cheeks and replaced them with a soft kiss. This is the mostlovely gift anyone has ever given me David, how can I ever thank you? David said, you already have. There are only three others on the TITO V that are allowed to wear these in public spaces, and they are King, Winston, and me. Welcome to our inner circle.

It was only weeks ago that A.J. was lying on the surgical table being readied to get his elephant trimmed. Now he is in the inter-circle of the Ghost Cartel thanks to David. Shit, he thought, how fortunate he was to be safe for the first time in his life without having to fuck for it. He did nothing but be honest about his life and treated people with the respect they deserved. While they continued their holiday on the islands, he spent almost all of his time with David. Sometimes other crew members would have drinks with him and casual friendships developed among many of the staff and cartel members. David protected his privacy, and the crew knew it. King kept a watchful eye on both of them because he did not want to overlook any warning signs like he did before.

Several weeks passed and they were growing tired of the Americans Paradise and decided to head out to sea again and their next destination was The Kingdom of Tahiti, the largest in the French Polynesian Islands. The 2300-mile voyage was well within range of the yacht, so the almost nine day trip was time again for all the crew to enjoy the breathtaking blue waters of the South Pacific. Their pantry and fuel at capacity would allow them a comfortable voyage south with the trade winds at their back.

A.J. and David would enjoy some of the secluded spots on the yacht where they would lie wrapped arm in arm, on soft beach towels, sharing more of their past lives with each other. David was always saddened by the hardships that A.J. had to suffer his entire life, just to live or stay alive. During their time together A.J. never made sexual advances toward David, even though he might have responded with affection. A.J. respected David so much he would do nothing to jeopardize his devoted friendship with him for any reason.

The third night at sea David and A.J. were having dinner in the main dining room with all on board when King asked A.J. how was his friendship with David getting along. A.J. said. Natural was his reply. Do you love him? King asked? A.J. looked David deep into his baby blue eyes and said, **"I love him with all of my heart"**. David said, King, I have never met a softer and more respectful man in all my life. He has

73

respected me sexually and emotionally every second since we met. He has demanded nothing from me or wanted nothing. All he shares is his honest soul every day. Spending time with him is my greatest pleasure. I used to be emotionally lonely but no longer, I feel like a complete man now.

A.J. pulled David next to him and kissed him on the lips in front of all to seal their relationship for the first time. King sat back in his chair at the end of the table and smiled, knowing the feeling of being in love for the first time. Like he did with Jim, his first love. A.J. and David got up from the table and returned to **their suite** to finalize their newfound love. When they entered David slammed the door shut, took A.J. by the hand and led him to their king-size bed. For the very first time in his life, he started taking his partners' clothes off starting with shoes, then his black tight-fitting shirt. When he got to his shorts then he looked A.J. into his dark brown eyes, seeking permission and A.J. gave him a nod of approval. Button by button he loosened his shorts which was difficult because his elephant had gone so large that the buttons became hard to unfasten. When the final button was plucked open his elephant fell out, because that morning he was wearing a pair of his bikini undies.

Laying there in all of his beauty A.J. rolled over on top of David. Kissing him on the lips again, he said let's take this slow. I want this moment to last forever. David said, I want you to make love to me with all the passion you have. A.J. removed his Polo Shirt and started kissing David's beautiful lips and neck. With such force he left a large mark on the right side of his neck. Working his way down to his hairy chest.

He quickly removed David's shorts and he was wearing black jockeys revealing his large virgin erection. A.J. buried his face in his jockeys, smelling his man scent. God, you smell like an angel, he said. I wonder what you taste like. David reached down and quickly removed his last piece of clothing. Laying naked underneath A.J., he pulled him tight against him and said, I am all yours. Take it easy on me, David said, remember this is my first time. Not to worry A.J, replied, you are with someone who is in love with you.

During the next several hours both of them climaxed several times, just by the intense passion. A.J. smelled every crack and crevice in David's hairy body. David, did the same to A.J. 's smooth milky way body right down to his toes. His scent was that of **"INITIO"** and exotic expensive perfume of the wealthy.

He remembered that scent when he was working as the assistant to the unnamed aristocrat in Spain.

Later that evening they both shower together and took a romantic stroll around the deck of the 250' TITO V, stopping briefly in the bar in the man cave for drinks before reclining on the aft deck to view the full moon in the sky over the South Pacific.

King and Winston didn't miss the opportunity to take full advantage of the romantic nights at sea either, King, since meeting Winston, had not been as sexually fulfilled since Jim's passing several years ago. Winston's passion keeps him overflowing with man juices of a twenty-year-old. Winton's tender and loving sexuality only matches his handsomeness. They were a perfect match he thought, and Winston agreed as they took turns passionately pleasing each other every night.

Capt. Oliver and Wayne, what a pair. Oliver had trained Wayne to navigate to yacht falsely over the two years that they have been together. Oliver, ten years Wayne's senior, kept Wayne challenged all the time. Mentally, physically, and emotionally. They were a great team. The Ghost Ship was in good hands as it navigated the high seas.

TAHITI AND BORA BORA

*T*ahiti within sight, Capt. Oliver called King and asked if he wanted to dock immediately or cruise the island's coastline for a picturesque harbor to anchor before docking at one of the busy ports. As they surveyed the coastline they were taken back to the black sandy beaches and the majestic beauty of the island.

Their first stop was a small village called Tiarei, where they anchored offshore. Visible on its shoreline were spectacular waterfalls and dense forest. It appeared to have many trails that if a person wanted to hike, they could spend a day exploring the thick vegetation. Chef Jeffery and Tommy and two cartel members, took the shore boat into town and fortified the pantry with fresh vegetables and exotic fruit only found in the Polynesian Islands, and the other two scouted to small villages for any sign of cartel activity.

King called Simon to the office and inquired if he would check if there was cartel activity in the Polynesian Islands, especially in Tahiti. As he always does, he contacted GYS Security Services in Miami. Then Capt. Oliver motored on to the secluded beach of Tikehau, with its pink sandy beaches and clear blue water perfect for snorkeling. King called a general meeting on the aft deck and informed all on board that Wayne would be available to run the shore boat for trips to the beach for them to relax and enjoy the privacy that this spot had to offer. Wayne ran shuttles in the morning and late afternoon taking ten of the crew ashore for their pink sand experience. Early that morning while some of the crew were being shuttled off the yacht, David instructed the staff to do a deep clean of the TITO V. During the next four days while they were anchored there the Ghost Ship was polished inside and out from bow to stern. On the night of the fourth day they cast off for the Northern Polynesian Island of Bora Bora only 120 miles north of Tahiti.

The Ghost Ship was so majestic and sleek it could vanish into the night almost undetected. Night cruising was the ship's favorite time to travel, as the water is calmer, and the winds are not as gusty. And by that time, most of the staff and crew are off duty to enjoy each other's company and have drinks on the aft deck under the stars. They call it **"The Bewitching Hours."** This is when the seduction begins and ends, and it can often be seen and sometimes heard in the hallways of the yacht, as it glides through the water of any ocean that it may be traveling.

It has been almost a week since David and A.J. declared their passion for one another. Little by little David shared some accounting details with A.J. Prior to doing that he consulted with King, just to ensure that his decision was sound. King instructed David not to provide details on their bank account locations around the world and the amount of money they had, I would however be okay to discuss individual unit operations which A.J. may be able to provide guidance on. David was relieved that he made the right decision once again. King began noticing a complete turnaround in David's manly being. His confidence, decision making, communication skills, and general swagger had changed so quickly he thought it must be the influence that A.J.'s had on him, which is a good thing. King was thinking to himself if the two of the were having full blown sex? But he really didn't want to know the answer to that question.

Bora Bora is so lush and beautiful Winston said, King let's stay here for a while. Okay, he replied, so

Winton called Wayne, the 1st Officer, instructing him to dock in that small town. When they were twenty minutes outside of the Bora Bora Yacht Club, Capt. Oliver called the harbor master requesting docking. They had but one cement mooring on the outermost part of the harbor. Oliver had no choice but to tie up to that mooring and drop a stern anchor to secure the yacht from drifting side to side. The yacht was all secured, the shore boat was lowered, and the shore boarding ramp lowered, everything was ready for a caravan of people to go into town.

That morning Simon came into the office and informed King that both Bora Bora and Tahiti were cleared of any known cartels.

Their current operations centers were located on the active drug shipment islands where cartels are located. King and Winston were relieved to hear the good news because they wanted to continue their R&R through the Pacific Ocean without any concern for their safety. David was in the office looking over their most recent income report and he noticed that NZ's income was on the rise again. He called Ian at their NZ location and inquired about the turnaround in net income.

Ian said the advice A.J. had given them was right-on. The big-time drug dealer that he referenced was the magic wand that fed them the information they needed to get back on track with their drug hits. They had made four takeovers in the last ten days, putting them back on the positive side for profits once again.

David shared the financial information with King and informed him of Ian's comment about A.J.'s advice about the drug dealer was right on and contributed to their improved bottom line figures once again. King sat back in his chair, looking out the window at the yacht club. Putting his hands behind his head he said, why don't we call A.J. up here and give him a pat on the back. Let's see how he responds when A. J. arrived, he was dressed in his short black shorts with that tight black tank top. He sat down next to David and said, "what's going on my friends?" David replied, "we just got our financials in from NZ. Profits are back up; in fact, they are out of the red and all losses recovered." Ian gave your lead credit for the new drug hits that resulted in the increased profit.

A.J. said good. Glad I could be of help. King got up out of his chair and walked over to A.J. who was sitting on the small settee and gave him a kiss on each cheek. A cartel kiss as one would describe it, A.J. with a big smile on his face looked at David and said, "Now don't get jealous he is not my type, he laughed. Winston did the same. David said it was my turn, come A.J. Let's go below, we have some business to take care of. I hope it's monkey business, A.J. replied.

After all their cheek kissing, David was ready and willing to show his appreciation for all the good fortune A.J. had brought to the Ghost. David took those black shorts off with one strong tug. The tank top A.J. peeled off himself. Naked on the bed he was ready and waiting for David's next move. David removed all of his clothing down to his black jockeys then sat and straddled his new lover just admiring his natural beauty. He took his hands and ran them on his face, neck, and chest. He could feel the elephant growing larger between his legs pressing against his manhole.

What a wonderful feeling. The feeling was all new to him. David said, "What now? A.J. said, "It's all up to you.

David said you are so big, what do you do with that monster? Anything you want, A.J. replied. "What are my choices, David asked. Come on David, use your imagination. We will let the reader do the same. To say the least, their night was a blissful mess. They had to shower for a long time to clean themselves, then changing the sheets was a must. As they were heavily stained. With fresh linen and scrubbed bodies, they went back to bed and slept through the night until late the next day. When they got up David walked gingerly to the bathroom to check for any visible signs from the night before, which there were none showing. Then he and A.J. got dressed and went to the dining room for lunch. When they entered the massive dining room all eyes were on them as if the crew members knew something they didn't. They both smiled at each other and took their place at the head of the table.

After lunch they, along with two bodyguards, one of which was Paul, took the shore boat into Bora Bora for an afternoon of shopping. David brought A.J. several new outfits and himself two new shirts. The four of them stopped for drinks at the Manuia Bar, a local gay hangout before heading back to the Yacht Club, which is also a gay friendly establishment, catching their shore boat back to the TITO V.

Back aboard the yacht, they headed directly to their suite. A hot shower to clear the perspiration from the humid day of shopping. Each of them standing face to face in the shower, caused David's hairy body to tingle with the desire from the night before. He looked at the elephant man standing in front of him with a sheer heat of desire. A.J. smiled and said, do you think you know how to make this elephant man moan for more? What do you mean David replied. A.J. kissed him. Then turned around putting his hands on the wall bending slightly at the waist and extending his white chocolate bubble butt against David's extended manhood and said, push it slowly into my cave where dreams come true.

When they were finished David almost fell to his knees in exhaustion. A.J. washed off with hot soapy water as did David and they both ran naked to the bed, belly flopping, spread eagle. They lay there for a long time just staring into each other's eyes, that is all the communication they need, at that very moment in time, to share the love they had for one another. David finally spoke up. No one could have ever told me twenty years ago that I would be in love with another man, especially a person like you.

King's lieutenants in the Caribbean and Winston's in Tonga had their cartel operation under control. The only aspect left to be managed was David's end. All of the money that flowed in, and when I say money, it is in the millions each month. David would continually say, we don't need any more cash. There is no place to put it. We can't spend it fast enough no matter how we try. King said let's triple our cartel and staff salaries. David said, yes, we can do that, but they don't spend their money either and there is a limited amount that they can accumulate without being noticed by the feds.

"Do you want to shut down one of the operations, King asked. David said, if we do, which one would it be? King said the Ghosts are so damn handsome. They are perfectly trained assassins; we can't lose them. David said, we can integrate them into your operation in the Caribbean Sea. They would really add some needed polish to that operation. The Caribbean operation cannot be transferred to the South Pacific, they are murderers not assassins nor polished enough to add value and there are too many of them. Why don't we sleep on our problem, David said.

And tomorrow morning, over breakfast, we can all discuss a strategy/plan. Sounds like an exceptionally good idea David King stated.

That evening when David got back to his room A. J. was just waking up from a nap and said, "What's going on? Looks like you have something on your mind. Does it show, David said. Yes, you have those questionable wrinkles across your forehead that show up when you are thinking about a serious topic. Well, get dressed, let's take a walk around the deck, I have something to run past your business mind. Oh, sounds serious, A.J. said. He got dressed in one of his new outfits that David had brought him the day before. Then they headed up to the top deck for a stroll in the warm night of Bora Bora. David said, we are thinking about shutting down one of our operations in either the Caribbean or in Tonga. You don't know anything about the cartel in the Caribbean, it is run by two of our top lieutenants Byron and Aaron on Marquis Island, which is south of Miami, Florida. When we retired to the South Pacific, we integrated that cartel into Kings Cutthroat Jamaican Cartel, and it is being run as the Marquis Cartel off of our island. There are over a thousand thugs in it, and they are thugs nothing like the Ghost. We make a large amount of money from that operation without any exposure. Tonga is where the exposure is. We make money which we don't need, and we are staffed with the finest of Kenyan men. The **"Black Magic"** of Kenyan men cannot be matched by any of our Caribbean tugs.

That is the issue I am thinking about. "What do you think you would do if it were your cartel, David asked. Another important fact, King rebuilt the Caribbean operation from the ground up when his former lover was imprisoned for money laundering, many years ago. And the two people who are in charge are his personal favorites and have been for decades. So whatever decision that is made will be a difficult one.

A.J. said first of all take money out of the decision. Then it all boils down to a staffing issue. Where can beautiful people get you the best results or new results that possibly you never thought about? If you sent the Ghost to the Caribbean, how could they improve the operation? They are so perfectly polished they can manage a unique operation, whatever they may be, to launder money or improve communication, in ways that you may not have thought about before. Once again, money isn't a priority, sustaining and embedding your cartel deeper into all the islands is the important factor.

You're correct. Ghosts can walk the streets undetected among the masses where current cartel members are there for one purpose and one purpose only, to kill or instill fear into our victims. The remainder of the ghost cartel who don't want to leave the South Pacific are so rich they can retire and live a life of splendor on any island of their choosing.

David said, here's another item we need to think about. We have five yachts fully staffed and we will need to relocate as well. But as luck has it, we own seven yacht clubs on various islands that could accommodate all our vessels, plus our own Island.

Maybe our business model should be, like you suggested, focused more on improving communication and looking for new above board business opportunities to clean our massive amounts of money.

The next morning at breakfast David had A.J. joined King and the other Winston in the man cave for the planning meeting. When they walked through the door Winston spoke up and said, "good morning love birds". David sat down at his desk and A.J. pulled up a chair next to him. King was first to speak up. Who has a plan that they would like to share?

Winston then said, the Tonga operation is so massive with manpower, and buildings spread over six islands in the South Pacific. Closing it down would be a giant undertaking. What would we do with five yachts and their crews? It just sounds so very difficult to achieve. Then there is the cartel staff, what do we do with them?

David chimed in. He said last night A.J. came up with this idea. Close the Tonga operation. By taking money out of the equation, the Ghost and their yachts and crews could be transferred to the Caribbean, we already own seven yacht clubs there. For those cartel members who do not want to leave the South Pacific, they are wealthy enough to retire and live a grand lifestyle. The Ghost assigned to each yacht club will be able to improve communications and look for new ways to establish legal businesses to launder the money we have stacked up, in various locations, that we can't spend.

Once again sitting back in his desk chair and gazing out the window and thinking aloud he said, that sounds like a very good idea. Improving communication, is a secret weapon that we have not used yet. To date, in the Caribbean, it has been bullets and intimidation that produced results. Now we need a way of handling our results. A.J. how did you come up with that idea when you didn't know our overall operation? A.J. replied, "I just took making money out of the equation.

A.J. went on to say, David told me once that he had so much money, he couldn't spend it all and if that's the case you need to clean it somewhere. The more polished people you have, say the Ghosts, operating in the port cities of the Caribbean, the more legal business can be established to launder the money. Just one Ghost can run and operate 5-10 businesses and you have ten Ghost Cartel. You're looking at a minimum of 50 businesses cleaning millions of dollars each and every week. I don't know how much money you have but the plan would work for any amount with the **Ghost**

Cartel at the helm. King said, let's sleep on this new information again tonight and until then let's cruise to Tahiti and check it out, we don't want to miss this island paradise while we are down under.

By nightfall the Ghost Ship was under way for its short cruise to Tahiti. Capt. Oliver secured docking at the Yacht Club De Tahiti for the 250' TITO V, with a panoramic view of the harbor and marina. When the crew got up in the late morning they found that the intense humidity had already built up to an uncomfortable level so everyone found refuge in the air conditioned comfort of the vessel's massive interior rooms. They soon discovered that this island was no different than any of the other South Pacific beauties that they had enjoyed so while the vessel was docked, it was refueled and the pantry filled to the brim with fresh supplies. King called all of his managers from each and every operation center and requested their presence on board the Ghost Ship for a meeting in two days.

Helicopters started to arrive carrying a total of 12 of their lieutenants from all of their Tonga operation centers around the South Pacific. Once on board they met in the air conditioned saloon for drinks and small talk until King, Winston, David, and A.J. arrived. David said, how was everyone's flight? They replied cautiously but with a positive smile. Ian then said, A.J., what a surprise to see you so comfortably fitting in aboard the yacht. David spoke up in his defense. Gentlemen, King is going to make a major announcement today that we made which will affect all our lives. The group now were sitting on the edge of their seats waiting for the other shoe to drop. But before the big surprise, let's have a drink, to celebrate. What are we celebrating? Ian inquired? You will soon find out, David replied.

The bar in the saloon bar had already been fully stocked by the Steward before their arrival. A.J. got David a diet coke and a double Hennessy on the rocks for himself. After about a half hour Daid stood up and said, we are going to reorganize our entire world operation. Every face around the table will be affected. We are closing down the Tonga operation alone with all of our operation centers in the South Pacific Ocean. There was a big "WHY," in unison, that sounded from around the table.

The reason is, we are making too much money and our biggest exposure or risk to bodily harm is coming from here. We don't need the small amount of cash generated by Tonga nor do you. King and I originally came here to retire and we did just the opposite, now we are going to do it again but in a different way. How's that Jamal inquired?

King said David told them the overall plan that you and A.J. came up with to safeguard them and make more money than we ever have. Jaali said who in the hell is A.J.? David said to my partner, "I suggest you and the rest of our cartel treat him with respect or you will answer to me. Are there any further questions about who A.J. is? It was as quiet as a collection of church mice around the room.

David said, "Now let's get on with it. All the yachts, crew, and Ghosts will return to the Caribbean. Any cartel members who wish to stay in the South Pacific may do so. You have enough money to live comfortably for the rest of your life. If you chose to return with your yacht, you may do so. King and I own more than enough yacht clubs on various islands to accommodate each and every one of our vessels. You, sitting in this room are the best of the best at what you do. We need to set up legal businesses on the islands to clean the billions of dollars and I mean billions of dollars we have already safely stashed away. By my projection, collectively, you the Ghost, with your polished communication skills and handsome features, can establish at least 5-10 businesses each. How much money can we clean in a month, no one knows, but it is sure more than nothing. Right now, we have it rotting in secret locations and vaults around the world. That is the plan in a nutshell. Questions?

When is this going to take place, Assir asked. King replied. When you fly back tonight, ready your vessels for a long voyage.

Announce to your cartel members their choice as I outlined and then one by one, we will head east, I will assign you your ports-of-call once you are underway. If you can't sell your operation centers, leave them behind. They are of little value to us anymore. Winston will take care of the Tonga operation.

After everyone had left the yacht, King and Winston returned to the suite and showered off the humidity of the sweltering day.

They were lying naked on their king size bed talking about the plans they had just made for their fleet of yachts and Ghosts to return to the Caribbean Sea. They were wondering if Bryan and Aaron could manage such a large and complex operation. They tossed the operation around in their head and decided to call David and A.J. to join them in their suite to further discuss the operational details of the plan.

When they walked in King and Winston were still on the bed undressed. Winston said have a seat on the sofa we would like to go over more of the details of your plan. Without getting dressed King and Winston sat on the two chairs opposite the sofa, with their masculine bodies fully on display. King asked, David, do you think our lieutenants Bryon and Aaron can handle this new operational plan plus their operation? No, not in the least. You selected each and every one of the ghosts. You understand their methodology. Our lieutenants can't relate to their mind set or skills. They are used to thugs not polished assassins. Assir and Jaali have done a great job of managing our operation in the South Pacific and they will do the same in the Caribbean once they get reorganized. I don't think we should set them up on Marquis Island. Their operation is entirely different. We need to pick a safe port for them to operate out of.

A.J. said, you two look like twins but a few years apart. If I had to give one of you a gold star rating, it would be a hard decision. **Hard** Is the key word. Ha, he said. David nudged him on the shoulder and said, let's get back to our room before you get us in trouble. They both got up, while they were walking out of the room Winston said, "you both are working your way up to the **"power couple"** of our cartel, in more ways than one. David just smiled.

Both couples wasted no time in making love and retiring for the night. David, while being attacked by the elephant man whispered in his ear, power couple, well if they only knew how powerful your elephant is, Winston won't call us a "power couple," I think more fitting would be a "smart and loving couple with immense power." Then they were spoon-fed to each other with A.J, wrapped around David like the coating of a corndog.

The first team scheduled for relocation is New Zealand, and was led by Antoine and Zachary. The 200' TITO XI, Captained by Frank, along with most members of their cartel, stayed on board for the planned trip to the Grand Cayman's, which was one of the money centers of the Caribbean Islands. David selected the Cayman's because Antoine and Zachery were the "Executive- Service '' team that replaced Ian & Cyprian protecting the wealthiest man in Nairobi. The Cayman's was a wealthy Island, and their yacht will be docked at the Grand Cayman Yacht Club, the primer yacht club on the island that they owned.

The TITO XI was the newest yacht of their fleet. So, no maintenance would be required for their 7800 mile trans-pacific voyage through the Panama canal to the Caribbean. Capt. Frank plotted his course via the Cook Islands, Marquesas Islands, then through the canal to the Cayman Island. The month's journey will be the longest that the Captain and crew have traveled together since joining the yacht in New Zealand.

When they arrived at Grand Cayman Yacht Club a 200' slip was waiting for them as the Marquis Cartel, owned the club for several years, had its cadre of attendants waiting to assist with the docking lines and to greet the new members to the Island in the Southern Caribbean Sea. When Ian & Cyprian appeared on the stern, they were greeted like royalty by Byron, one of the two leaders that King & David had charged with their prized Marquis Cartel operation in the Caribbean.

Byron was "shocked" when he saw Ian & Cyprian, as to their handsome qualities. Just the opposite of all of their cartel members in their entire operation. Ian said, come aboard Byron, I will introduce you to our crew and staff who live on board the TITO XI.
While Ian was conversing with Byron, Cyprian called a crew meeting on the aft deck. After a quick drink in the man cave, Ian, Cyprian, and Byron joined the gathering on the back deck.

Once again he was amazed that this was the Ghost Cartel. David shared the plan with them and the others when they arrived.

But what I can say is that they are closing the Tonga operation in the South Pacific. That is a complete surprise, Byron said. Right now, we only have on board 4 cartel members who are polished assassins as we overtake freighters and take their drug shipments. Two couples retired very wealthy men and relocated to a remote island in the Oceania group in the South Pacific. The other two couples wanted to continue with us, for another great adventure.

I can't wait for Cyprian to meet you. We have our own plane, traveling by boat is too dangerous for us, so I am going to call him and have him fly in tonight, if you don't mind. Not in the least, you are well to stay on board, we have plenty of room for both of you. Two suites or one? One will be fine, Bryon replied. By dinner time Cyprian had arrived and joined everyone at the dark African black wood dining table for a late meal. Both leaders of King & David's operation in the Caribbean were introduced and a question-and-answer session period continued throughout dinner. Ian & Cyprian's black and sophisticated manly features spoke of unusual qualities that were lacking in the Marquis Cartel.

The next morning, the four leaders met in the office on the top deck of the TITO XI and placed a call, on their secure line, to the TITO V, which was still in Tahiti. David outlined their plans for the new businesses they were planning to establish in the Caribbean. It would be managed separately from the Marquis Cartel. King informed them, at this point in time, the manager had not been determined and until that decision was made, each location would be self-managed with the assistance of Byron, Aaron, and their cartel.

Aaron said, "I am glad King didn't close our operation, Byron and I would be out of a job. There isn't a chance in hell that we would fit into your Tonga operation, you guys are not polished enough. Ian laughed, well behind the scenes there are people like yourself that get the dirty work done for us, if need be. Well, that is a downright degrading commitment Aaron said. Ian laughed again and said, I mean, not everyone looks like us. Does that make you feel better?

Aaron and Bryon took the rest of the day to meet the four cartel members left on board. He listened to how they overtook drug shipments, repackaged them, and sold them at a discount to small drug cartels on the South Pacific Islands. They made money, but not the profits that their operation makes in the Caribbean. But here there is always exposure to the DEA, FBI, and other agencies plus other cartels from Mexico and Central America. So, it is always a cat and mouse game to survive. And unfortunately, their cartel had been **"marked for death"** several years ago, like a jenks one could say, so every day it was a fight for survival.

By the end of the fifth month all of Ghost Ships were relocated to their designated yacht clubs in the Caribbean.

TITO X Montego Bay Y.C. - Jamaica

TITO VIII Royal Jamaican Y.C. - Jamaica

TITO VII Marina Y.C - Dominican Republic

TiTO XI Grand Cayman Y.C, - Cayman Islands

TITO VIIII Georgetown Y.C. - Cayman Islands

At this point the TITI V, with King, Winston, and David had returned to Catalina Island to spend another quiet Christmas and New Year's while planning their next trip, where east, west, or south, the direction was still undetermined. The holiday planning this time was grander than the time before. They learned from their last visit they had to order all of their supplies several days in advance because of the infrequent deliveries to the island.

Being only 30 miles from Avalon Harbor to the Port of Long Beach, they decided to go to the mainland to resupply and complete their holiday shopping. They planned to stay in port for only six hours, so David and A.J. set up ground transportation for all crew members who wanted to complete their holiday shopping list, while Chef Jeff had called ahead with the food order that was ready when they arrived in Long Beach.

Since the TITO V came in from Catalina, it did not have to go through customs inspections or integration. What an accidental choice it was to stop on the island before heading to Long Beach. A lesson well learned for the next time. After five hours everyone was back on board. Under the cover of darkness, the Ghost Ship slipped out of port, headed back to the island and its moorings that were reserved.

On board the TITO V were all of the former members of the **"Thunder Boys",** Winston's cartel members, who were assigned to Tonga. we're being returned very wealthy to his San Diego organization. In fact, Winston had just promoted two of the Tonga co-leaders in his cartel. Standing alongside King, "no matter the direction or destination he travels, I am by his side," Winston said, By the end of January, the Ghost Ship was on its way to San Diego. Capt. Oliver circled out in International waters for a long period of time until their shore boat could transport all of the Thunder Boys safely back to the city. Then King instructed him to return west to San Clemente Island which is used by the Navy and Coast Guard. There are about 200 military and civilian personnel living on the island but it is not accessible to non-military civilians.

King told Oliver to find an anchorage on the west side of the island because the Navy Seals use the east side for their swim training between Camp Pendleton and the Island in its Shark infested waters. Capt. Oliver found a fifty' shallow reef and anchored it. Setting a "Spring Line" at the stern to keep the yacht steady into the wind, now all set for a temporary stay at the island. The sound of incoming and outgoing jets takeoffs and landing on the island was their only disruption but soon they got used to that sound which they referred to as "Top-Gun Music."

King, Winston, and David were still undecided where to go. Their fleet of Ghost Ships were all located in the Caribbean and it was time to set up businesses to clean their billions of dirty money.

Each one of their leaders polished to perfection, needed a strong leader to validate action plans. Time was wasting, they thought, collectively what should they do? A.J. spoke up and said, is there a small island that we dock at or can purchase another yacht club to safely hide while they supervise their new business ventures.

The four of them scoured the map of the Caribbean. A.J. said, how about the two small islands in the southern part called **"Trinidad & Tobago"** are independent countries. Not part of the United States judicial system and the DEA. FBI, and other agencies won't be patrolling. Port of Spain on Trinidad is a rough and tumble port city, and our cartel can handle those challenges. In fact, we may be able to establish an **"Executive-Service"**

Security Business Company or two in which we can clean some of our cash.

Another great idea A.J., King said. You are becoming an invaluable asset to us. David saved your life for two reasons, and we know what they are, **"for love and money,"** as they say. I can't put my finger on how much money you have made us so far, but I know it is in the millions. King, I have never had a home or a family in my life that I can trust with my life. I have found one. I am going to do everything I can to make our family stronger with what I know. I know the streets, let's say I am street smart and book smart combined, just like you King, you surround yourself with people who are skilled with talents you don't have, that makes you a stronger King, A.J. stated.

David said I am learning a lot from you A.J. in both areas. My life was missing passion that triggered many decisions that I made. Now I am making direct decisions instead of giving advice and that is a complete change of character for me, isn't it King? It sure is David, I haven't seen you this decisive and happy in all the years that we have been together. But I want you to know one thing, I will still protect you with all my resources, just understand that A.J.   King, A.J. said, David is protected with all that I have learned to survive on the streets during my entire life, so between the two of us, he is protected better than any gang member that I have run into in the South Pacific. King told Capt. Oliver to plot a course for Trinidad and the Port of Spain. The 4000-mile trip was the maximum range of the Ghost Ship. A refueling stop needed to be identified before arriving at their final destination. After their 30 day trip they arrived at Trinidad's Port of Spain and secured a 250' slip at the Trinidad & Tobago Yacht Club located on the north-west side of Trinidad Island. The Ghost Ship was the largest and most present vessel in the yacht club of Trinidad. It drew the attention of everyone. A line started forming on the long pier to view the yacht. It grew so long that it extended through the gate and down the winding street. Capt. Oliver called the harbor master requesting security to control their gawking patrons. In about an hour, armed guards appeared on the ship side and encouraged viewers to return to the dock located 100 yards back from the TITO V.

That evening, all secured at the dock, Chief Jeffery knocked out their first meal while not at sea. Lobster obtained from Trinidad's local fish market with sweet potatoes and greens. Warm apple pie with a large scoop of ice cream also from the local vendor served for dessert, with a pie crust that melted in your mouth. After dinner, the crew collected themselves in the saloon for drinks. King asked his 4 team of cartel members who lived on board, what they thought about establishing an "Executive-Service" Security business like his lieutenants on his fleet of Ghost Ships, who were trained in Kenya? Jamison said, "Count Stephen and me in on the new business venture, as we are already trained to serve at your request.

"EXECUTIVE-SERVICE" SECURITY BUSINESS

*A*ll of the leaders of the South Pacific operation out of The Kingdom of Tonga were skilled in the security business in Kenya. "Executive–Service", is a specialized skill trained to provide protection to wealthy individuals, diplomates, or assist in the prevention of kidnapping or locating those kidnapped. Its members are skilled assassins who could blend into a crowd or vanish into the night undetected to complete their mission. They worked as a gay couple, who fight to the death to protect their client and each other.

A.J. the idea about establishing the business is well founded because of the security risk that all people, in the above-referenced risk group, are faced with each day on all islands in the Caribbean. Each yacht that was relocated to their designated island carried two already trained security personnel from Kenya. Now it is time to train additional teams to provide the specialized skill. King put a call into Assir & Jaali, his leaders who selected all of the Kenya personnel, to inquire as to the training time necessary to bring all of the Ghost up to speed on the skills necessary for their new business venture? Jaali replied that it would be better to train them in Kenya, where the service is highly in demand. They would be able to assign each team/couple to an expert in the service and there are schools that are also available. Kenya and some of the East Africa countries are where the highest demand is, for this unique service.

David requested A&J (Asstr Jaali) to provide them with a list of trained and to be trained security personnel, then they would decide who to send for training. King instructed A&J, who's vessel was the last to pass through the canal, to head south to the country of Belize. Belize City had a travel warning for Americans citizens to use caution if going there. A security business would be ideal in that country but to locate it in the south because most of the residents there are of African descent and his ghost would blend into the crowded marketplaces and business communities easier. Capt. John and the TITO V from Tonga made their voyage north from the Panama Canal to Belize without incident. They found dockage at the Placencia

Yacht Club at Placencia Caye. I small and unspoiled Caye north of Belize City. King thought it would be a perfect location to set up one of their new business ventures.

Also, Belize is only 500 mile to the Cayman Islands, which was an easy voyage in either direction for the Ghost Ships.

David received the requested list of trained and to be trained security personnel. They had fourteen fully trained in Executive Service and 20 that requested training. Assir & Jaali reached out to their Nairobi contact, who replaced Tony & Marc, his last two who he selected and who were replaced by them and were still protecting the richest man in Nairobi. He informed them that he had 20 partially trained individuals that he would like to send to Kenya for advance training in Security Services.

They were pleased to hear from him. Where are you? He said in Belize, in the Eastern Caribbean. What are you doing there, they ask. My team just returned from the South Pacific and are setting up a Security Service throughout the islands. An entirely new business venture for us and that is on the right side of the law.

As in Kenya, money is always an incentive to get results. Assir said he would wire you $200,000 US dollars if you guaranteed that they received the best of the best training in the shortest period, but he wanted the highest of results. They replied, $250,000 and 30 days and they would guarantee the results, or all the money would be refunded. Jaali said, how about half upfront and the other half when the training is completed. You have a deal my friend.

David and A.J. review the list of candidates. David knew all of them by name but A.J. I just looked at their files. He was very experienced at reviewing paperwork to evaluate people. He only question four of the twenty volunteers:

Sam - 5'7", long blond hair, blue eyes, and bodybuilder

Miguel - 5'8", braided hair, medium build, quiet

Fred - Black, 6'3", slender, size 14 shoes, long fingers

Chris - Black hair, mustache, white, medium build

"What do you think of these four A.J. asked David. David replied, "I have known every member of our cartel since they joined us.

Remember we started from nothing in the South Pacific. King approved all of them and I am not one to question King's approval. He is like you, he grew up on the streets of Jamaica long before either of us were born. I guess he knows what he is doing then, A.J. said.

Assir & Jaali have made arrangements for their training in Kenya. We are paying our source handsomely for a quick 30-day intense course in Executive-Service, so we need to make travel arrangements for them to Kenya right away. How are we going to get them there, A.J. asked? By private jet out of Piarco International Airport, here in Trinidad. We will have them all take a helicopter to the TITO V and will fly them direct to Nairobi. Our contacts will meet them there and after the training is complete, we will fly them back. Sounds like you have everything under control David, A.J. said. Let's go to our suite and take a warm shower together to wash off the stress, it has been a long day. David said, oh what a relief that will be to have you wash me up and down. My stress will flow down the drain as your beautiful elephant leaves its trail on my back. Is That the plan A.J. said. Let's get the move on and get out of this office.

When they got back to their suite there was a mad dash to remove each other's clothing. A.J. won the race. His elephant was ready for action. David, fully naked body was waiting impatiently in the bathroom for him to enter. A.J. had removed his PSD underwear revealing his handsome smooth body and he turned the shower on and when it was just the right temperature, they both jumped in to begin their soapy wash down. David lathered his hands loaded with the finest soap that the Ghost Ship stocked, and later A.J. 's body from head to his feet, leaving his groin area last. His pubic hair, now fully grown, was so masculine he couldn't resist lathering it up with more soap than usual.

When he did, pre-come began oozing out of his fully erect manhood. For the first time, David kneeled down to remove all of it with his soft lips. It had an unusual taste that David thought that he could be addicted to. A.J. was so excited as to David's soft lips on the tip of his elephant, that he exploded then and there, with such force that David's face was covered with the white cream.

A.J. raised David up and licked the cream off his face and tasted himself, for the very first time.

A.J. finished washing David and they each towel dried each other. Running to their bed in heat A.J. threw David down on his back and caressed hairy body gently leaving no part of it untouched. David spread his arms and legs far apart so A.J. would not miss anything, then rolled over and told him to enjoy himself to the fullest. They both were so tired after their long day they went to sleep on their silk sheets, wrapped like cocoons before the butterfly hatched.

The next morning two by two all twenty of the ghosts arrived on the TITO V to catch the charter flight to Kenya. They were so excited to be part of the new "Executive-Service" detail that they were dressed in their finest clothing to make sure the right impression would be made on their contact in Nairobi. The flight was over 26 hours, and the charter jet had a fuel capacity to make it non-stop. When it arrived, their contact was waiting at the airport and transported them to the finest hotel in town to recover from their jet lag. Two days later, each pair was assigned to their respective trainers and the 30 days intensive "Executive-Service" training began.

David and A.J. began identifying the island's cities so that their new businesses would be established. Some of the locations did not have yacht clubs, so private offices would need to be established. A.J. suggested we need a business address for all of our locations to make it legit. We can't operate them off of the Ghost Ships. Your right A.J., and that will also give us an additional right- off. When the guys are all fully trained, we will have 17 security teams, totaling 34 ghosts. Now we need to identify the best and most profitable island cities that we can use to provide services to.

David asked King and Winston to meet him and A.J. in the office. When they were all together David explained to them that their new business should not be run off of their yachts but rather ligament offices on the island cities selected for their new business ventures. They also suggested that they should brainstorm other venues that could be provided out of the same office to launder more cash. King said, let's give that some thought tonight and to meet again in a couple days to gather our collective thoughts.

King and Winston came up with the idea that they have many cartel members who could provide security for shopping centers, stores, yacht clubs, and other venues. One individual could handle each assignment without having to send a team to perform the service. They could triple or quadruple the fee they charge the client and launder some more of their cash. If they charged the client $1,000 they would deposit $3-4,000 for their service. Small amounts add up, they said.

A.J. came up with private charter service between islands with their 10 "go-boats" that each yacht carried on board. At their speed, they could connect close islands, for VIP clients, in minutes. That fee would be large. Applying the same formula could bring in tens of thousands of dollars a day.

Davis said, if we could connect with "go-boats" why not establish a small "air charter" service between islands that could carry up to 6-8 passengers. But we would need trained pilots and planes that we don't have now. A.J. said, we can run the combined services, "boat, sea, and security" out of the same offices that we establish on the selected islands. The air service would require a major capital investment because we do not have the planes. Pilots can be trained if we hire the right person to manage that division.

In just two days King, Winston, David, and A.J. had come up with services to get them started on their new business ventures all over the Caribbean Sea. As in the past, David will be assigned the responsibility to complete the research for the best islands to establish each business and identify property to buy/ lease like they did in the South Pacific. This time he decided to use the help of Winston & A.J. to complete the gigantic task. Winston & Simon, head of security, would be assigned the responsibility for "Security", A,J, "Transportation" air-sea, and he would research buy/lease options. King would use his influence to close the deals, in whatever way necessary, as the locations are identified.

NEW GHOST CARTEL

*K*ing & Winston now relaxing in their polo robes, tucked safely away in the grandeur of their suite on the TITO V, could not resist the pleasure of consummating the sexual bliss of the "power couple" of the Caribbean Sea. Their combination of strength and cartel manpower was unmatched except by the Mexican Cartel located on the landmass of the peninsula of Central and South America, which they avoided at all cost. King admitted, while holding Winston loving in his grips, that he was the sexual energy that he needed to restore his cutthroat leadership power for their new empire.

David, only months ago sat alone in his suite completing his bookkeeping and accounting tasks. Now emotionally involved, for the first time in his life, with another individual that he was "in-love" with, A.J. had appeared out of nowhere in the South Pacific to save David from a life of loneliness.

A.J., whose entire life was one of lying, cheating, running schemes, and doing whatever it took to survive, was now safe next to David. For the first time in his 28 years he was learning that truth and honesty can provide security and wealth, and money cannot buy happiness or love. After all of these painstaking years he found what he was looking for, "passion", the tigger for deep sexual desire in another individual, who was now David, his soulmate.

From the surgical table, where his elephant was going to be trimmed, to the king-size bed with black silk sheets it had been a scary journey. For him to achieve such unknown trust and honesty, his complete story is yet to be told.

Beauty & the Beast as King & David have been referred to, have been together for 20 years or so. traveling from the Caribbean to the South Pacific and back again leaving a trail of money, blood, death, and passion in their wake. The only sound you hear is the "Ghost Ship" cutting through the waves of the high sea.

The TITO V now docked in Trinidad and Tobago, deciding to use this island location as its headquarters, to coordinate all of the new business ventures in the

Caribbean. Combined with its helipad and the island's airport, they had the air transportation hub necessary to cover all of the islands .

David along with A.J., now combining their brain power, worked endlessly to identify islands on which to establish offices/storefronts for their businesses. They knew in some locations they would have to provide housing for its cartel members because they didn't own yacht clubs on the island cities. They consulted with Winston & Simon as to what additional security would be needed to provide protection in these remote island cities.

David asks A.J. to identify as manager of flight operation for their "air-charter" operation. The individual must be certified flight instructor and with a culture to fit into their operation. They also must have the intelligence to know which aircraft to purchase and maintenance. A.J. check with flight training schools from all over the world. He identified "Executive Flyers" a small but dually accredited school in a remote key off the eastern coast of the Southern Florida. He asked David how he should interview the prospective candidate. David suggested he should conduct a phone interview with all the instructors and then they would go over the list with King to determine their next course of action.

In the meantime, he and Winston discussed security measures for their remote locations. Winston said, once the locations were identified and purchased/leased he would ensure at least two cartel members were assigned to each under the umbrella of their new "security division."

David consulted with King on the island search. They agreed that it would be best to stay away from establishing offices in USA territories, such as the US Virgin Islands, Puerto Rico, and to use extreme caution dealing with Cuba.

David's first list contains the most dangerous islands of Jamaica, St. Kitts, Bahamas, Haiti, Dominican Republic, and where they were docked at Trinidad & Tobago. For the time being he left Cuba off the list. Then he listed islands that they could provide for the air, boat, and security business for:

Grand Cayman

Anguilla

Antiqua

Saint Martin

Barbados

Grenada

Martinique

Aruba

Bonaire

Curacao

Turks & Caicos

Belize

French Guiana

Saint-Barthelemy

He went over the list with King and Winston. King said, shit David are we biting off more than we can chew? A.J. said, we can start small and expand as we go to perfect our services. You're right about that A.J. You are really good to have around, King said.

A.J. smiled as if someone was tickling him with an Ostrich Feather, then turned to David and gave him a big kiss on his cheek. A.J. had never felt so appreciated in his entire life.

The training of their "Executive-Service '' team in Kenya was almost finished, only one more week to go. A.J. identified three flight instructors from Florida to be interviewed for their flight services division. David, King, and Winston went over the resume for all three individuals, Joie was identified as the top candidate to be interviewed. He was 29 years old, black, had been training for over three years and certified in fixed wing aircraft that land on land and sea. He spent a year in airline maintenance training which the other two did not. King suggested that we fly him to the Trinidad and bring him aboard the Ghost Ship to meet the team and see how he feels about the business we are planning to establish in the Caribbean. If we make him feel uncomfortable, we can tell right away that he is not a fit for our new position. I will take care of it, A.J. said. In four days, Joie landed at Trinidad's airport and was met by Simon, head of Security. He introduced himself and quickly drove him by armored limo to the TITO V docked at the yacht harbor in Trinidad. In the meantime, Simon had run a security background check on Joie, which came back flawless.

Joie, whose body language was tense, revealing concern and distrust, boarded the "Ghost Ship" looking around at the yacht's grandeur every step he took. When he and Simon enter the man cave, A.J. got up and introduced myself as the contact person who he had spoken to and had made all of his travel arrangements. Then he was introduced to King, Winston, and David. King inquired, how was your trip from the Key's? Joie replied, it would have been much better if I had flown my own plane, I loathe commercial airlines. David said, maybe the next time you will chart your own course and **the sky will be yours to conquer**.

King said, Joie, the four of us in this room are starting several new venues here in the Caribbean Sea. One of them is an air transportation division consisting of as many land and sea planes as it takes to meet our needs. We do not have any knowledge in this area. That is why you are here. We are looking for a person with your qualifications to head up that division. Joie asked, how many islands and planes? King's reply, "that is where you come in, as manager of the division, you would have authority to assist in island selection for flight shuttles between islands and the purchase of all aircraft. Also, your division would be responsible for maintenance of the fleet of aircraft.

You're looking at a major capital investment," Joie said. Do you have funding secured for all business ideas or they are dead in the blue water of the Caribbean before you start? Funding has been taken care of for all of them. What are the new businesses that are in the planning stage at this time, Joie inquired. King said, they are in two categories, transportation, and security. At this point, does this management position sound like something you would be interested in, A.J. asked. I have a very secure position in the small flight school where I am at today. I only work about 25 hours a week and make enough money to live on, since I am not married and share a beach bungalow with another instructor. I have a pretty kick-back lifestyle, Joie said. Maybe you can bring your roommate along and find a good position for him or her in the organization, A.J. said. It is a he, Joie said.

While you are thinking about all of this new information Joie, have you ever been on a 250' yacht before, King inquired. Yes, I have, Joie replied. The Keys have several mega yachts and many of their owners have private planes and pilots that I have trained.

The yachts arrive in the Keys during the winter months and leave before hurricane season. I did notice when I boarded, yours does not reflect a name on the transom, which I find unusual. Why is that Joie asked? King replied, that is why it is referred to as the "Ghost Ship." As you noticed, it is all black with silver streaks and we can vanish into the night, oftentimes undetected providing all on board a sense of security as we travel the high sea. Clever idea, Joie stated. We have 5 more just like this one but different lengths, now currently docks at the yacht clubs we own in many of the port cities in the Caribbean, King stated.

What is it that you do that can afford your company six mega yachts and has the capital on hand to start all these new businesses. It has to be illegal, Joie stated. At this time, it is not of concern where we got the money but the new businesses we are planning are legal and we want you to run it that way, King replied. David and A.J. take care of the financial end of the business. Who will manage "Security," Joie inquired. King replied, Simon, who is currently head of our own private security. It is almost dinner time; our steward will show you to your stateroom so that you can freshen up and change after your long trip. Afterwards, he found his way to the very large saloon for drinks, then they all gathered in the dining room for dinner.

They were just finishing their dessert after a delicious dinner that Chef Jeff had once again prepared, and a helicopter landed on the yacht's helipad. Ten handsome well-dressed men jumped out, crossed the deck as the second chopped landed and ten more equally handsome men got out and in no time they were all gathered in the saloon next to the dining room. Joie inquired as to who all these men were. Simon said, part of our newly trained "Executive-Service" team, who just returned from advanced training in Kenya. Kenya, Joie questioned. Yes Kenya, Simon replied. That is where the service originated. Our team just finished a thirty-day intensive course and will soon be assigned alone with others to our Security Division.

A.J. asked Joie if he had given any more thought as to their planned transportation division. Yes, I was unsettled until I saw the investment you made in training your security team. You guys are dead serious about all of this. You are focused, prepared to train, well-funded, flexible as to locations, and the way it sounds will give me the authority I need to make the air transportation happen. I would like to let you all know one thing about me before we go any further, I am a perfectionist, I don't do a half-ass job on anything I do. They went around the table agreeing that perfection is a good thing but sometimes adjustments or compromises need to be made to get the results. Joie agreed that he is a team player. He said that he would like to discuss the idea with his roommate in Florida before making his final decision. But at this very moment he liked the business model.

King asked Joie how he planned to hold the discussion with his roommate? By phone, in person on the yacht or fly back to the Keys for the discussion? I think it would be best to charter a private plane then he can fly here himself. He needs to meet everyone to understand the scope of the operation and the leaders that we would be working with. Done deal King said. A.J. helps Joie make it happen. Oh, by the way, what is your roommate's name, Simon inquired. Devin, Joie replied. Simon's background check on him came back without any exceptions.

In two days, Devin piloted a Twin Turboprop plane from the Florida Keys. Landing at Piarco International Airport in Trinidad. Simon and Joie picked him up in the armored limo for the short drive to the TITO V. Devin was equally as handsome as Joie and it was very clear that they were close friends. As before they met in the man cave on the second level of the yacht. King made the introductions around the room and the overall new business venues. Joie, discussed in detail the air transportation plan with Devin and that if he took the position as manager of the division, he would like Devin to join him in some capacity, yet to be determined. Devin simply replied, Joie, wherever you go, I will go right along. We have been together too long to break up now.

Their plan sounds like a new adventure for us. Joie looked at King and said, we are on board. We can fly back to the Keys and get things in order and within the next two weeks will be back to start the planning process. A.J. jumped in and asked, can't one of you handle closing down the Keys and one stay here to immediately start to work planning the air transportation business. Devin and Joie got up and walked out of the saloon to the outer deck to discuss the plan and when they returned, Joie said, I will stay here and Devin will handle Florida's issues. OK, A.J. said.

Let's all take a night off with the rest of the team and get to know each other. You two will be working with a group of individuals that have been together for years and most of them are partners, hope that does not bother you. Devin said, it definitely won't. On the yacht that night there were over 50 cartel members from all over the Caribbean. They gathered on the large aft deck and spent the night drinking and talking under the stars of the Eastern Caribbean. Many of them had to spend the night sleeping on deck lounge chairs as all of the staterooms were filled to capacity.

That night Joie and Devin enjoyed each other's company in the privacy of their plush stateroom. Both of them were handsome black men, about the same age and height of 5'10" with slender bodies. A.J. had found the right couple to head up their new air-sea transportation division. In the morning, Devin returned to the Keys flying the same Turboprop, to close down their operation and gather up their personal items. Within six days Devin flew back to Trinidad to join Joie and they were ready to start the planning process for the new transportation division.

The most dangerous islands in the Caribbean were identified by Simon and King to set up their Security Service:

Jamaica - owned two yacht clubs

Dominican Republic - owned two yacht clubs

St. Kitts -

Bahamas -

Haiti -

Trinidad & Tobago - where the TITO V was docked

Joie and Devin identified 50 primary islands for air/sea transportation, but in reality, they could provide any Caribbean Island with private air-boat charter service. They Decided to headquarter this division on Grand Cayman, a British Territory, and where the cartel also owns a Yacht Club. A yacht club would be beneficial because it would have space to dock several of their "go-boats" between runs. Grand Cayman would also provide a maintenance facility to ensure that their aircraft and boats were always in top running condition.

To keep it extremely simple, King and David combined the headquarters for both operations on Grand Cayman where they already had several bank accounts and a respected relationship with local leaders of the business community. After several days of intense work Winston suggested that the six of them take a break and have Capt. Oliver chartered a course out into the blue water of the Caribbean to give the staff and crew some well-deserved rest away from the dangers of Trinidad & Tobago. First Officer Wayne, located a small uninhabited island by the name of Rock Island, not far from the yacht club where he could dock.

Early the first morning, they anchored on the eastern side of the island which blocked its view from the mainland of Trinidad.

Chef Jeffery and Tommy, once again prepared an outrageous brunch which spread the entire length of the service bar on the aft deck. Two by two the crew and cartel members filed into the very large, covered area to enjoy their brunch. Tommy stood by making individual requests for Omelets, Mimosas, Bloody Mary's. David and A.J. arrived together, dressed in matching white shorts, deck shoes, no socks, and yellow tank tops. Devin and Joie surprise everyone when they arrive holding hands, wearing only swim trunks, looking as if they had just had a pillow fight.

King and Winston had called Chef Jeffery to have all their meals delivered to their suite because they had no plans to get dressed or make an appearance out of their five star suite for the entire day. During the last four weeks their time had been devoted to the new organization and they needed to make up for the intimacy that they had physically missed during that period of time.

David and A.J. had slowly become a one man show. They were dressing alike, walking alike, talking alike, and sharing passion alike. Each one of them was surprised as to the depth of love that was being formed deep within them. David told A.J. many times when he was wrapped in his arms and looking into his dark brown eyes that it was like looking into the window to his soul.

And each time he became more handsome than the time before, Devin and Joie were childhood friends. Their relationship grew like a flower. From a seed, well-watered, to a mature plant with flowers that never quit blooming. So flagrant, each giving off a man scent with more passion every day, that needed to be explored.

Since the Grand Cayman was identified as the headquarters for their Security & Transportation operation David needed to locate two offices to operate out of. He did not want to combine the two into one office for security reasons. George Town, being the capital city, its airport was very busy receiving hundreds of passengers daily who were traveling to other remote islands in the Caribbean Sea. A perfect location for their transportation venue. "Go-Boats" can take people to the closer islands quickly and the sea planes could take off on land at seven major island airports and on many of the further island, which do not have airports, can perform water landing and dockage and reboarding can be completed on the piers at the remote island locations.

Simon needed to select a person to head up his security division, because he was head of security for the TITO V and permanently assigned to King and David's detail. He knew instantly who he wanted, Adam, his part-time companion from GYS Security, that he had worked with several months ago. He placed a call to him on Adam's private contact number in Miami. When Adam answered, Simon said, who is my part time bed pardner holding up without me? Adam, on the other end of the phone, just laughed and said, I am lonely as hell.

Simon gave Adam a quick overview of the project and asked him if he would like to come to the Cayman Island to manage the operation for the cartel. He said, I will be on the next plane out of this humid state of

Florida, see you tomorrow. Where are you now, he asked. Simon said, Trinidad's only yacht club. Okay, Adam said, I will be there before you know it.

A.J. & David were in the man cave enjoying their morning cup of java when Simon pulled up, dockside, with Adam. When Adam got out of the armored limo his long blond hair was blowing in the wind and his tanned muscular body stood equal to Simon's. They boarded the Ghost Ship and went directly to the office where King & Winston were waiting for them. King and Adam gave each other a firm greeting and King introduced Winston to him as his new life pardner. Moments later David and A.J. walked into the office and Adam was shocked to see that David was toting a new companion by his side, an event never seen before during Adam's time on board.

King said, it is great to have you back. I am glad to hear you have agreed to manage our new security business. David popped in and said, Adam, I missed you, but I don't think as much as Simon. He has been all business, no play since you left. Hope you can bring him back to life for us, he said. Adam asked, who is this handsome black man you have with you David? A.J. replied, David saved my life in New Zealand, since then we have grown together as one. I can say, I am living each day as if it is my last. And that statement by A.J. is very close to the actual truth.

Adam said, Winston it looks like you got a promotion from your San Diego operation. Well Winston, when I look into King's eyes there's that special sparkle that wasn't there before. You must be the torch that reignited it. Could be, he said. King said, you are very observant.

You had a long trip Adam, why don't you and Simon take the rest of the day off and retreat to his stateroom and relax, if you know what I mean, we can get together later tomorrow to discuss the security business. They both left without hesitation and when they entered the stateroom the door was quickly shut and locked.

Sounds like thundering horses could be heard down the hallways for hours as the two made up for lost time since separating several months ago.

During the next week while David & A.J. were starting their search for offices and in some cases residences on the islands that they had identified as "highly dangerous," Simon & Adam spent time reestablishing their relationship with the newly formed "Executive-Service" members, consisting of over 17 teams. They would be assigned on a first come first served basis to the highest paying clients, on the most dangerous islands. Their large service fee will then be quadrupled falsely after the bill was paid and then deposited into their legitimate banking accounts.

David & King had already purchased yacht clubs on two of the six dangerous islands, Jamaica, and the Dominican Republic. They agreed that it would be safe to use their own personal yachts for the team's residence. Only four islands needed offices and private residences for their team. Puerto Rico Island, which is an unincorporated U.S. territory, was one of the islands they needed to establish a foothold because of its danger. All bills for their services must be deposited through banks on another island without U.S. banking relationships.

The last three islands St. Kitts, Bahamas, and Trinidad & Tobago (where the TITO V was currently docked) would need office and residential housing. David & A.J. searched for several days to provide Simon & Adam with a listing that would safely satisfy their security needs.

King asked David to begin the process of assigning their yachts to island locations all over the islands beside where they owned yacht clubs. The TITO V, the headquarters yacht David suggested being docked in Antigua-Barbuda in the Lesser Antilles. That island location was very safe and was located outside of the U.S. banking regulatory system, so David could process all of the necessary money transfers without red flags being raised.

Besides that, it was a beautiful paradise to explore, and its people were charming and friendly.

The 210' TITO XI, he recommended, be located on the Saint Martin Islands. The north side being French and the south being Dutch it could travel between port cities to provide support for their transportation hub or security personnel if need be.

The 175' TITO X they located on Saint Vincent Island. It was surrounded by Grenadine Islands with many small port cities, again where their security or transportation hub could be serviced.

175' TITO XII they decided would dock at Anguilla. A very small British Territory comprising several smaller islands. Idea for air/sea operations.

200' TITO VIII, Barbados, an independent British commonwealth nation in the eastern Caribbean. Providing once again security for financial transfer of funds and an ideal location for their multitude of services.

150' TITO VIIII would be located on the Cayman Islands to manage the Security Business. It was small enough to cruise in and out of ports undetected, when called upon. Joie & Devin would be located in Little Cayman where they would manage the Transportation Business. They located a bungalow with a small pier for a seaplane and "go-boat" that could connect them quickly to any island in the Caribbean.

TITO V was still docked at Marquis Island where Bryan and Aaron were headquartered running the Cartel Operation in the Caribbean. The profits of its operation were still being reported consistently.

Now with all yacht assignments complete, Adam and Simon flew to the Grand Caymans to personally look for a villa to house them while coordinating the Security Business. They located a 5br/6bth 6500 sq ft. Villa, with a private beach coastline extending one half mile. It did not have a pier, but their "go-boats" could easily dock on the sand. The purchase price was $6,950,000.00. Small change for such isolated beauty and with such serenity. Simon asks David to purchase the property. After it was purchased, King authorized construction of a 250' pier that would accommodate any yacht in their fleet. They employed all the dockworkers available on both islands in the Caymans and the pier was complete in thirty days.

Their Security Service was now ready for operation. Adam went to each of the most dangerous islands and met with local authorities. His company "S&A Security Service, provided a wide range of service from personal protection from kidnapping prevention, kidnapping retrieval and location, bodyguards for high profile individuals and dignitaries, and any protection required by individuals who wish to remain anonymous. The authorities on each island were more than happy to have their resources, as they were either unstaffed or their staff were taking payoffs so that criminals could elude the authorities.

After two weeks, Adam had established 16 accounts on three of the most dangerous islands which netted them several thousands of dollars a week. Simon was more than pleased with his lover's ability to network their new business throughout the islands. The eight teams who were providing the Executive Service received rave reviews, in fact, one team already saved the life of one client in the matter of one week. Within 2 months all Executive Service teams had been assigned and now the only assignments left were the individual assignments for stores and shopping centers, etc.

David told King that money was flowing in from Adam's operation without a hitch, and Simon had selected the right person to head up that division. King said, let's hope we are as fortunate with our transportation venue. King inquired if David had been in touch with Joie as to the progress, he is making on the purchase of sea planes and aircraft? No, I haven't, David replied. I am going to have A.J. follow up with Joie if you don't mind, he told King. I have been transferring money hand over fist and I have to be very careful because some of these islands have dual banking relationships, meaning they run money through U.S. banks and foreign banks at the same branch. It takes careful planning on my part on each deposit. I understand what King said. Yes, have A.J. manage the transportation venue.

A.J. was so excited when he was told that the transportation hub would be under his supervision to set up. That would be his first real opportunity to show his new cartel that he can and will be a valued asset, not just a bed partner to David.

Little Cayman Island was an ideal location for their transportation venue because it had a small airport and two docks on either side of the island which could be used for Seaplanes. A.J. thought one dock could board passengers and the other could be used for mechanical servicing for watercraft that were unable to land at the small airport for routine maintenance.

RETURN TO MARQUIS ISLAND

*W*hile Joie and Devin were finalizing their search for aircraft, King gave Capt. Oliver instructions to chart a course to Marquis Island. He and David hadn't seen Bryan & Aaron for years. The only communication they had was their money deposits of profits, which continued to grow annually. The walls of his mansion were still filled with cash that needed to be cleaned.

When the Ghost Ship was 50 miles from the island, Capt. Oliver called Bryan to let him, and Aaron know to alert security personnel that they would be docking in a matter of minutes and to dispatch two "go-boats" to safely escort them into the harbor. Simon didn't want to take any chances that the authorities would be patrolling the waters around the island. The ship had left Antigua under the cover of darkness and traveled over 1000 miles, timing its arrival at Marquis Island at midnight.

When they docked Bryan & Aaron were there to welcome their leaders back to the island. The TITO IV was still docked there, looking as new as the day it was purchased several years ago. King went down to the transom and asked Bryan & Aaron to join him & David on board. They went directly to the man cave and ordered a round of drinks. They were laughing and reminiscing about old times they shared together when the four of them were on the island. Soon after a couple drinks, two distinguished men entered the room. King and David jumped to their feet and one by one introduced them to Bryan & Aaron. Winston knew them both from the party he attended on the island in remembrance of King's previous lover's passing. David introduced A.J., as his pardner, who he met in New Zealand and is currently heading up one of their cartel's new operations in the Cayman Islands. Bryan & Aaron were both pleased to see that their leader, King, was back in the world of love and happiness. They knew for a fact when King was in love, he would accomplish the impossible with a softer touch. As for David, that was the eighth wonder of the world. Never have they seen him in love with anyone other than Jim, King's deceased lover or King, his protector. God only knows what happened to him for this emotional love affair to blossom.

Bryan & Aaron would never question either relationship because it brought their leaders back home to the Caribbean from the South Pacific.

King said, we made the 1000-mile trip back to the island because I left a few things in my mansion that I need to retrieve. He said, Winston and A.J. Come with me, I will need a helping hand. Also bring along those four "Louie Vuitton" bags in our suite, will you please Winston. When they entered the mansion Winston & A.J. was captivated as to the lavish luxury that was contained within its fortress-like exterior. King led them down winding stairs that seemed never ending until they reached a large room with gold plated weapons of all kinds and a large oil painting.

They both inquired who the handsome man was. King replied, the first love of my life. Then King placed his lips on the lips on the picture and it opened like a vault door. When they walked into the room it was filled with $1,000.00 bills floor to ceiling. They carefully filled each bag as full as they could. When they returned to the Ghost Ship, King had them put the bags in the medical room on the bottom level of the yacht. Then he locked the door and returned to the man cave to rejoin his guest for another round of drinks.

King took Winston for a tour of their Island and a walk on the beach, which reminded him of the many times that he and Jim had walked to its beaches hand in hand. He knew that Jim would be pleased that he had found love again and that his peaceful state of mind was ruling the cartel. Winston asked him if the island brought back many unhappy memories and King replied, no, only loving memories. Just like today King said. I am so in love with you, I am happy to share our island together. David's visits to the island were only for business. He would spend his time alone on board the yacht doing his paperwork and resting. His boring lifestyle was being protected by his platonic lovers King and Jim, then Winston. For a time, he had given it all up and exiled himself to Spain, when Jim was imprisoned. Upon Jim's release, he located David. Immediately, David returned to the Ghost Ship to be loved and protected once again by his two protectors.

After King's visit to the mansion to fill the "Louis Vuitton" bags, he gave Capt. Oliver orders to return to Antigua where he would have David intermingle the millions of dollars along with their legitimate earnings that they were flowing in from their newly formed Caribbean operation.

Small lands and sea plans were identified that would meet the planned transportation venue. The idea was to keep the number transported small, between 4-6 passengers, thus catering only to VIP clients. That way the fee charged would be higher and the island locations more remote. They would basically service any island in the Caribbean, either by plane or "go-boat" which ever provided the best and fastest service for their client. The "Go-boats" could only carry up to 6 passengers at top speed of 100 miles per hour. The fastest service of any of their competitors. The average cost for each plane was between $750,000-$1,000,000. Their initial investment would be over $14,500,000 for 10 planes and 5 additional "go-boats". Joie ran the investment cost past David, who was surprised as to the amount of money they would have to spend but they had more than enough cash for the capital investment. His only concern was where to buy the planes because they could not pay cash for them with companies that deposited cash in U.S. banks. David helped Joie locate airplane sales/leasing companies worldwide.

David located a company in Spain by the name of "Planes Unlimited." They would build any small VIP plane land/sea to the specification of the buyer.

David instructed both Joie & Devin to fly to Spain and discuss their specifications with the builder. When they arrived, Kevin met them at the airport and took them to the Madrid factory. On display were several models of aircraft that were under construction that were exquisitely designed and had the latest safety features.

They sat down with their design team and went over their needs for the most beautiful aircraft that they could demand top dollar for in their planned flight services. The designer came up with ten land and sea planes that were as plush as the Ghost Ships. In fact, they would be painted in the same coloring as the yachts, black with a silver streak. They submitted the renderings to A.J. for approval. He in turn reviewed them with King & David just to make sure that his decision was in line with the overall business plan. When King saw the pictures, he was overjoyed. King gave David a big kiss on the cheek and said, so far you have made a very wise choice in saving the life of that cartel rat. He said, every day A.J. is securing his position in our cartel by his own well-deserved actions. Not in the bedroom but in his contribution, which is the real measurement. Action speakers louder than a fuck, that has always been my bottom line.

David asked A.J. to meet him in their suite. When A.J. walked in David had already showered and was sitting on the sofa in his robe with the biggest smile on his face. By his side on the table was a double Hennessy on the rocks. A.J. said, what's up my love? David said, why don't you take a quick shower while your drink is cooling? Then put on that white robe that makes you look so richly dark. A.J. returned quickly. Standing just outside the bathroom door in his robe, David had never seen him look so relaxed and happy. Just stand there for a second, will you please A.J., I want to adorn your masculine black beauty, David said. He went on to say, I have never in my life loved anyone as much as I love you. You are an incredible person who has yet to reach a full understanding of what our life will be like together.

Come over here, sit next to me, and enjoy your drink. When he squeezed in next to David, he reached down and opened David's robe to reveal what the gods had made and saved for him and him along for all these years. This virgin man, so smart, kind, understanding, trusting, and sexy, how could he have been so lucky, he did not know. David laid his head on A.J.'s lap, feeling AJ.'s elephant swelling to the touch of his head. David opened A.J.'s robe. The man's scent was so strong it filled both nostrils with the scent that David could never resist. Not a word was spoken. Unbelievably David took the lead that night and his actions that evening is yet another story to be told.

In less than 30 days 5 of the 10 aircraft they ordered arrived from Spain on an extremely large freighter that docked offshore in the Cayman Islands. The planes were offloaded and the pilots that Joie & Devin had already trained, flew them to their assigned island location. In a very short period of time transportation services were in operation producing revenue that exceeded expectations. When the pictures of their planes and boats reached the marketing outlets, rich clients were booking weeks in advance for flight/boat services. In fact, some clients had a permit booking every other weekend when they visited their beach houses on their private islands. When the final 5 plans arrived, their service was already booked well in advance. Joe and Devin's business was a skyrocketing success and a mega money cleaning machine for the former cartel.

That night, when Joie & Devin retreated to their exquisite bungalow on Little Cayman Island, they looked out over the blue waters of the Caribbean, totally naked and embraced in each other's arms. Remembering the days when they were pinching pennies to survive. Now they had servants at their beckon call, meals were ready for them, and they were totally in-charge of their own personal destiny for the first time in their life. They always thought working for a cartel was a bloody, cutthroat environment. That was not the cast working for King and David. The Ghost Cartel is the most prestigious gay cartel in the world of cartels and especially in the Caribbean Sea.

ATTACK ON THE GHOST SHIPS

The Ghost Ships were docked all over the Caribbean. Some at the cartel's own yacht clubs and some at ports-of-call. They hadn't been threatened by any other cartel sense returning to the Caribbean Sea. They have purposely stayed out of the drug end of the business and are now focused on the laminate businesses to launder the billions of dollars they have stockpiled over the years. Their bank accounts were now being filled with spendable income that could be deposited through any U.S. bank.

The headquarters yacht, the TITO V, has been safe from attack since returning from the South Pacific and its crew and cartel members have enjoyed the rest. All their personal relationships have blossomed and grew stronger. King and Winston spent most of their days rooming the many decks in their swimwear, getting darker by the day from the Pacific Sun.

David now had to send little time on the books and bank deposits as he had trained A.J. on some of the accounting procedures which came naturally to him. The two of them were just natural together. Nothing false or make believe. A.J. never forced anything on David that David didn't want to experience sexually. One could say everything was perfect.

All of the Ghosh Ships, in their relaxed state, cruised freely in any direction of their choice. Their yacht's security systems were often left off or ignored because of safety that had surrounded them since their return. Refueling and resupplying was done at various ports throwing caution to the wind.

Assir & Jaali who was the head of their "Executive Service" team from Kenya that was formed in the South Pacific, was still living on board the TITO V. They were not as comfortable with the lack of security that prevailed on the yacht. They understood the biggest strength any cartel has is **surprise**. They met several times with Simon, the head of security and voiced their opinion to the effect. He ignored every warning.

One morning when the 175' TITO XII, one of their smaller yachts, left its Anguilla dock for a leisurely cruise around its many islands. It headed north to explore the southern Cuban coastline. Capt.

Phil plotted a course that kept the yacht safely in International Waters. For weeks now they had not been threatened by any hostel cartel so he left all of their warning systems off, only relying on him and his first officers visual observation and the radar which would identify vessels in the surrounding waters. When they were passing the southeast corner of Cuba a rocket landed within 5' of the TITO XII bow. Capt. Phil made a hard turn to his stern then proceeded in a zigzag cruising immediately at full speed. He turned on all of the yacht's warning systems which revealed that the yacht was under attack from land, sea, and air. He sounded the alert for all crew to report to their defensive stations then placed a call to King on the TITO V.

Simon was informed of the attack. They did not have any other yachts in the immediate area to come to their assistance, so Simon called Joie. He instructed him to pick up as many cartel members as he could, fully armed with automatic weapons and fly them to the area where the TITO XII was being attacked. He instructed Joie to encircle the attacking planes and ships using their high-powered weapons and blow them to extinction.

Capt. Phil estimated that he could be out of range of any land threat within minutes, by running the yacht at full speed. But the "Go-Boats" they were using had snuck up from a couple smaller islands while their security system was off. And their boats were fast. Antoine and Zachary, head of security on the yacht had trained their security detail with precision. They each manned their automatic weapons located on the bow and stern of the vessel and without any fear for their own personal safety, stood for what seemed like hours, and sank aircraft and go-boats as they became within range of their powerful weapons. When Joie's planes arrived, automatic weapon fire could be heard for miles and exploding boats and planes crashed and sank into the Pacific.

King asked Joie to fly over the area and see if there are any survivors bobbing in the Pacific and if so fly them to his location in Antigua He flew exceptionally low encircling the area for a few minutes and spotted three men attempting to stay afloat. He landed his seaplane and retrieved them and reported back to King that he had three on board. Good King said, how long will it take for you to fly here?" Joie said, 4 hours. I will land at the dock, and you can transfer them to your yacht for integration. King replied, I will be waiting.

King and Winston had not been in their cartel mode for months. Being in a relaxed state of mind for so long they both thought that they didn't want to revert to the blood and guts of their previous life. They summoned Assir & Jaali to the office. King informed them that Joie would be arriving shortly with three survivors of the cartel or whoever attached their yacht off the coast of Cuba. He needed to know who was behind the attack and if they could get the information out of them without killing them first?

Assir & Jaali, being trained as they are in Executive Service said that it would be no problem. They had done this many times before when getting kidnapping information for their clients in Kenya. They said their techniques are a bit primitive, but they work. King said, I don't care how you do it, all I want is who was behind the attack.

When Joie arrived with the three prisoners, Assir took them to the surgical room on the bottom deck. When the three of them saw Assir & Jaali they knew instantly that these two very tall, black men were skilled in techniques that they were unfamiliar with.

Jaali said, we are going to make it easy on you, who is behind the attack on our vessel? One of them said, we don't know, all of us were told by an anonymous communication to formulate an attack to sink the yacht and to continue locating them one by one until all were eliminated. What country are you from, Jaali asked. What cartel do you work for, Assir asked. No answer. Assir asked again, what cartel do you three work for? Still no answer. Jaali said, you the little, short fagot looking one, up one the table, as he grabbed his arm and guided him across the room as the other two were tied to their chairs opposite the surgical table.

Assir strapped his naked body down with several long ropes. Now I am going to ask you one more time, what cartel do you work for? Still no reply. He informed all of them that they were from Kenya where techniques for getting information from people are very painful, do you wish to continue with your silence, he asked. Still no reply.

They put the guys' feet in the stirrups of the table as if to inspect a woman's vagina. With Assir on one leg and Jaali on the other they began to stretch them out very slowly. They stopped briefly to tape his small dick to his stomach, then proceeded. His tiny ball sack was hung up in the air by a thin rope to the frame of the table so when his legs were stretched, his balls were tightened.

When he was stretched far enough to expose his asshole, Jaali got acid out of the cabinet and put it on the tip of his cock. When he did it ran down to his balls and all that could be heard was the scream of pain and by looking at the melting of skin around the foreskin of his uncircumcised cock.

The guy on the table passed out in pain. Jaali went to the medicine cabinet and got a bottle of adrenaline used to restore individuals with heart conditions. He gave him a double dose in a shot to his butt. His consciousness was immediately restored.

They guy looked down at his bloody cock and said, I can't give you any more information than I already have because the three of us are just mercenaries that follow orders for a cartel out of Panama.

Jaali said, so the cartel is out of Panama. Yes, he said. Now we are getting somewhere. I think if you know it's Panama, you know what cartels there are in Panama who would like to have us out of the way. Assir stretched his legs further apart. His other cartel members were sweating profusely, on their chairs, tied up against the wall on the other side of the room. They were shaking their heads to tell the guy on the table not to reveal any more information.

When they made the final stretch, his asshole was wide open. Waiting for an injection of truth sermon. Assir said, we are giving you one more chance to tell us the cartel's name, then we will make it quick and clean. No pain if you know what I mean. The guy on the table said you are going to kill us anyway so go ahead, you will not get any more information from any of us. Jaali said, we will see about that.

His asshole looked as if had been penetrated by something large before. It was twitching open and shut by just the nervous condition he was now in. Jaali looked around the room and found a funnel and inserted it into his hole as deep as he could get it.

The guy moans from pain or pleasure when it was inserted. Once inserted, Jaali took the same acid and raised it over the guy's head and centered it on the funnel, said final chance. No reply.

Drop by drop, the acid was released into the funnel, running into his asshole. Within moments he was screaming so loud that he could be heard all over the lower decks of the yacht. Jaali only released it a drop at a time, knowing that each drop would dissolve his internal bowel lines permanently and his death would be slow and painful.

The guy laid there taking each and every drop as a good soldier of his cartel. He passed out. Jaali did not retrieve him this time. His body was removed from the table and placed in a body bag. The next one was placed in the same position on the table, but a different technique will be utilized this time.

The second cartel member said, you will not get any more information out of me, so make it quick or slow. I am a dead man either way. Jaali said, how would you like to disappear from the face of the earth, a very rich man, and never be heard from again. I can make that happen. The guy said, there isn't anywhere my cartel can't find me. So, you know who the cartel is. Let me assure you Jaali said, we can make it happen. Our connections are so vast that you and your pardner can virtually vanish. We can guarantee it. Do you want to gamble with your life?

They both said where and how? We are both from Kenya, a beautiful country with people as handsome as us. With the amount of money that we can provide for you both, you will live like royalty for the rest of your life. We also know people there who will protect you from any danger. I can only assume that you are into both men and women, they will bring you pleasure there. The village men are so handsome and untamed. Each of you can have one of your own. Do you want a few minutes to think about it before we continue with our unpleasant integration? Yes, they replied.

Jaali and Assir left the room and went up to the office where King and Winston were sitting. King said, what's the scoop? Jaali said, so far all we got was that instructions came from a cartel out of Panama. The first guy provided that information but unfortunately succumbed to our integration before any more information was provided. The last two are considering an offer I made. What is the offer Winston asked? Jaali said. To be exiled to Kenya, with all the money necessary to live a lavish lifestyle for the rest of their lives and to be protected by our connections there. In turn, they will provide us with all the information on the cartel hit.

That is an outstanding offer. Let's hope they take it. Jaali said we are giving them some time to think about it. How much money are we talking about? King asked. Jaali said, in Kenya you can live like royalty on $2,000.00 a month. I thought if we gave them a million dollars and they wisely managed it, they could live a long time. If additional funds were needed, they could contact Assir or I through our connections there and we could replenish their bank accounts. Make the offer, King said.

Jaali and Assir returned to the operating room, on the lower deck, and walked in and the two said, we will take the offer. Ok, Jaali said, now spill your guts. They said the hit was ordered by the same cartel that killed one of your leaders a few years ago, when they were trying to leave Panama. They have been waiting for years to track your operation down and to eliminate your ships one by one until they get to King. The cartel has plotted and planned each move very carefully, not to be detected. Using various informants on all the islands to track your whereabouts.

Now Assir asks, how can we eliminate this threat?

That will be a challenge. I would suggest using your Marquis Cartel thugs to sweep all the islands and identify them. Because they have just arrived on many of the islands and came to be recognized by the locals that are loyal to your operation. Once they are removed, Panama won't be a threat because they will only have resources there. If you want to make a clean sweep of it, go back to your Panama Yacht Club in full force, now that you have seaplanes at your disposal and set up a trap for them. The leader is Little El Chapo, who is power hungry and stupid with perceived manpower. His men are devoted to him for some reason, just like we were, because it is either loyalty or death so what's the choice.

Jaali called King to the surgical room to hear the information firsthand. It was no surprise. It had been a long time coming and he knew one day that he would have to eliminate that little prick, El Chapo, which should have been eliminated a long time ago. King asked, is there anything else we should know? One of them said yes. El Chapo hates your guts. Your cartel has cost him a fortune and he wants payback. King said, Jaali will take it from here, you are on your way to Kenya, both very rich men.

Assir untied them from the chairs and led them to a small unused guest room down the hall on the lower deck where they could shower and freshen up. He provided them with a fresh change of clothes and told them that transportation will be arranged for their trip, first thing tomorrow morning. Jaali called Joie, to charter a jet to take their guest to Nairobi, first thing tomorrow and to advise him of the departure time.

The next day they both board a jet bound for the capital of Kenya with a million U. S. dollars deposited in a special account that David established for them. When they landed one team of the Executive-Service members were there to meet them and escorted them to an exclusive residence. It was already leased for them in one of the picturesque tribal regions of Kenya. They were both instructed that bodyguards were at their disposal 24/7 and a manservant was already on duty in their residence. They were amazed that every promise that was made for the information, was provided so quickly and as agreed. Now it was time for them to enjoy their life together, safely secluded from the cartel lifestyle, the hope forever.

LITTLE EL CHAPO - PANAMA

$\mathcal{K}$ing made a phone call to Bryan on Marquis Island. He asked him to put the call on the speaker phone so that Aaron could hear the information at the same time. When they were both on the line, he informed them of the information that he got out of the two cartel members that they had integrated on board the TITO XII after it was attacked off the coast of Cuba.

They were informed that Little El Chapo from Panama had been plotting for years to eliminate their organization vessels one at a time until King was eliminated. He wanted Aaron and Bryan to gather as many of the 1,000 members of his cut through gang as he could. He is putting a plan together to eliminate El Capo in Panama.

King said, we still own the Panama City Yacht Club. Remember when we bought that club, the owner told us that we were **"marked for death."** I guess he knew then that the Little Guy controlled his harbor. We are going to change ownership very shortly. King continues, the TITO IV is docked at the Island and with our new party color it can slip into Panama Yacht Club undetected.

He asked Arron and Bryan to formulate a plan, to be ready to move the 900+ gang members to Panama. They could use all of the planes they owned now that landed on the water. They could hold a maximum of 8 cartel members at a time. Making numerous trips during the night, they should be able to move over 100 gangsters. Also, they could use the entire fleet of yachts to move their team to countries close to Panama where they can take "Go-boats' ' to their assigned location.

Aaron said, we will start pulling all of our men together immediately. We have more than a 900 now, shit I don't even know where they are all assigned. It will take me a couple weeks to get this lined up. King said, get started, I want this bastard out of commission. Bryan put a call in to all his top lieutenants on all of the islands in the Caribbean. He instructed them to send all their men to Marquis Island. The Island was massive in land size but lacked housing for that many so Aaron had some of his men set up large tents in the jungle foliage area, which would be hard to detect by plane or boat. Facilities were brought in to provide toilets, showering, and a massive portable kitchen was set up. After two weeks the Island was buzzing with cartel members from all over the islands.

One after one their yachts pulled up to the dock and loaded as many members as they could hold to be transported to remote locations close to Panama. The TITO IV departed fully loaded with weapons and ammunition of all shapes and sizes. Capt. John knew of the past danger of the Panama Yacht Club and was very careful in plotting his course to enter it. Capt. John chose to enter it from the north end instead of the south, as he had done when King's lover, Ron was Killed.

Seaplanes took off night after night. Landing in remote beach locations on the Panamanian coast. They then formed hit squads made up of 50 of their cartel members, heavily armed waiting for further instructions as to where to go, from Simon and Adam. The TITO IV docked without notice at their Yacht Club loaded with over 500 cartel members that immediately dispersed themselves around the perimeter of the club. Simon and Adam had flown to Marquis Island to head up the security detail and coordinate the attacks.

King and Winston remained on the TITO V in Antigua so as not to raise any suspension on their cartels movement. David and A.J. stay close to King for their safety, as they were not as trained as their fellow cartel members were. It appeared to all of them that detailed plans were taking place for Panama. In less than 6 days they had to move almost 1000 of their gang to Panama and positioned them strategically around the entrance to the yacht club and all the roads into and out of Panama City. There was no way anyone, after arriving in the city, leave without facing an onslaught of firepower from the Marquis Cartel.

Now the plan. Simon had one of the yacht club employees who was loyal to their cartel make an anonymous call to one of El Caypo's cartel members informing them that the TITO IV was docked at the yacht club. Little El Chapo took the bait. It wasn't long before he and about 100 of his men started to enter Panama City and were heading to the yacht club. El Chapo was in the fourth armored vehicle. Once all the vehicles were in the city, all roads were sealed off with cement barricades. Spikes were scattered all over the highway and hundreds of Marquis Cartel members lined the streets to cover every possible escape route. When El Chapo reached the yacht, it sat empty, tied to the dock. Once he reached the yacht two green flares ignited high in the air. El Chapo knew instantly that something was up. His men surrounded his armored vehicle and began retreating the city.

Every road they took was blocked. Spikes blew out their tires making their vehicles stop in their tracks. Marquis Cartel members used rocket launchers to pierce their armor plating and their passengers jumped out and began firing only to be shot where they were standing. El Chapo's bodyguards escorted him to what they thought was a safe location on a small side street. They hide in the corner of an alley waiting for the automatic weapon firing to stop, but it went on for what seemed like hours.

His men were running and bleeding in all directions. He hid like a caged rat about to be slaughtered. When the gun fire stopped, he sent his men down the street to see if it was safe to retreat, but they never returned. He sat there, pissing his pants when 4 of the Marquis gang walked up with their automatic weapons in hand and shot him between the eyes and dragged his little body into the street.

One of the Marquis' gang members called Simon and told him that they had just executed Little El Capo and they would bring his body back to the TITO IV. On their way back hundreds of El Capos' gang members were scattered dead along the streets of Panama City. They had accomplished their goal. Revenge for Ron's death and Jim's imprisonment had taken years to complete but it is now done. Thanks to the two members of El Capos cartel that were exiled to Kenya for the rest of their life.

After the execution of Little El Chapo was completed, and his cartel was no longer a threat they restored their presence at their yacht club in Panama. King and Winston were so pleased with Bryan and Arron coordination of the attack that they gave them each $1,000,000 dollars as a reward to establish a nest egg for when they chose to retire and the title to the TITO IV for another retirement gift.

Not one member of the Marquis Cartel was killed or injured in the attack on El Chapo's' cartel in Panama. It took several days for them to return to their base of operation in the Caribbean. This time Joie chartered larger jets to take as many as possible in one load instead of many smaller flights like they did before.

Once their manpower had reached their final destination and all of the business were back in full operation, King summoned all of his lieutenants to TITO V for a celebration of their well-organized victory in Panama.

Devin & Joie arranged for helicopter transport for them to land on the headquarters yacht, docked Antigua. When gathered, Chef Jeffery had prepared a magnificent dinner of caviar, ribeye steak, garlic mashed potatoes, fresh sweet peas from the local vendor, and apple pie for dessert. The dinner lasted well into the late evening. When finished, they all gather on the large aft deck for drinks.

It was during this time when King & Winston appeared carrying several large boxes, one for each of their trusted Cartel Leaders. Ian & Cprian, Mbinga & Kaikai, Lankenua & Jamal, Antoine & Zachary, Tony & Marc, Kaelo & Abaui, and the founders of the **"Ghost Cartel,"** Assir & Jaali.

All of their Kenya cartel members remembered the time when King interviewed them when they were newly appointed to their positions. His method was always with a **"handshake and a kiss."** So, to test their loyalty and sexual comfort in being a member of his gay cartel. All of them knew the loneliness and hardships that King had suffered to maintain control over the cartel, oftentimes sacrificing his own love and happiness for the good of all. Today with Winston at his side, he is a softer man from the years past and the two of them shadowed by his long-time love David, are surrounded with the best team of Cartel members you can find anywhere in the world.

King, asked for their attention. Before passing out the gifts, he asked David to introduce A.J. to the group surrounding the deck. Winston, joining hands with King, said, you are our handsome **Black Magic Ghost** from Kenya. I have always placed all our trust and faith in your loyalty, skills, and swiftness that you possess. You have always completed every mission without fail. You all deserve more than what we are giving you today. We all want you to show our appreciation to you for **"mission accomplished."**

The four of them started handing out the 12x12" box around the deck. When each person opened their package, they found a **GOLD-PLATED GLOCK 45,** with the name and date they were inducted into the Ghost Cartel. Also, inside the box were ten $1,000 bills. Being from Kenya, where poverty is commonplace, they, while being employed by King, have lived a life beyond their wildest imagination. Now tonight, all any of them could do was to give their life once again to protect the cartel first, their pardner second, and their life last. They all got up from their chairs and knelt down and in a worshiping motion, gave King the best Kenya offering they could.

That night all of the ghosts scattered around the TITO V and reaffirmed the love for their pardner. David and A.J. stayed up very late, in their suite, talking about the first time they met and how their relationship had gradually developed through trust and passion, which today they enjoy so much. They both agreed, neither one of them would have guest months ago from the surgical table where David saved A.J. from a sure death, until now, that the long trail of passion leads them to the strong fulling sexual bond that today they had for one another.

The next morning, Chef Jeffery prepared individual breakfasts for each couple when they arrived in their dining room. Then Joie made flight arrangements for cartel members to return to their respective islands. By the end of the day all guests had departed the headquarters yacht and work was back to normal. Cleaning thousands of dollars a day through their legal business on the islands of the Caribbean Sea.

THUNDER BOYS IN SAN DIEGO

$\mathcal{W}$inston's cartel in San Diego had self-managed itself for the last several years. It was turning a small but study profit but nothing like when Winston was at the helm. Winston & King were looking over the last profit reports from its operation and the figures were not acceptable to Winston's. He called David & A.J. to the office and asked them to analyze the last year's profit reports and to determine what was going on.

A.J. took the lead in reviewing months of financial data, including incoming shipments received from their Mexican contacts and further distribution points in the United States. Net profits declined gradually month by month, unnoticeably, over the last two-year period. But year to date they were large, in fact in the millions. The volume received from its wholesale was consistent, but profits deposited on deliveries grew gradually smaller by 3%.

A.J. went over all of the detailed findings with David, who reverified the information to ensure that it was correct. Then they pull bank deposit slips. On their Monday and Friday deliveries of each week, with the same amount of drugs, the deposits were significantly lower. Winston had a 14-member crew that made the runs between cities from San Diego to points north. Winston had set up a system of rotating drivers on each run so as not to draw suspension by the authorities.

When A.J. was reviewing the bank accounting records he discovered that the same person was making the run every Tuesday and Thursday for the last two years and the deposit were getting small on the same amount of drugs shipped. All there was on the deposit slip was the initials **M. O.**, which identified the person depositing the money.

Having the information at hand, David called Winston to meet him and A.J. to go over the information that they discovered in their audit. When Winston looked at it, he said, shit, that is Michael Owens, he has been a member of my cartel since I formed it. I find it hard to believe. Winston placed a call to James, the highest-ranking member that he left in-charge, in San Diego. He asked him how things were going and if there were any problems with ships and profits being deposited from their operation. James said yes, we are down over a million dollars since you left but I can't seem to identify the problem. We still have our original team in place, so that hasn't changed, and product flow has been consistent.

Winston asked if he has been rotating drivers on a regular basis? He said yes, except for James who has a relationship that he wants to be home on different days, so I let him change the running days on Tuesday and Thursday to give him a longer weekend off. So, James, you approved this change, do I understand you correct? Yes, I did Winston. Have you audited his bank deposits? No, I didn't feel the need to because Michael has been with us for years, so I trust him.

Winston said, I think it is time that King and I paid you a visit. He hasn't seen our operation firsthand. I am very proud of it, and he has asked me many times to meet you. So, let's make it a surprise visit, okay? Sure, James said. We will see you soon, Winston said, keep up the good work.

After Winston hung up the phone all four of them, in the office, collected their thoughts and started planning how to handle their visit to San Diego. Winston asked A.J. would you like to go to San Diego first and tag along with Michael on a couple runs and witness him making his deliveries and bank deposits. Winston asks, your appearance will blend in with our team, being of Creole descent, you shouldn't have to worry about your safety. James will assign you to the runs on a trial basis to see if you are okay as a new member to join "The Thunder Boys."

A.J. said, that would be an honor. When do you want me to leave? Winston said, in a couple of days, let me get things ready on my end. The next day Winston called James in San Diego and told him that he found an individual by the name of Author who he thought would be a good addition to his organization. He was going to send him to San Diego in a couple of days to shadow Michael, their most experienced driver, on a couple runs to see how he fit in. James said, I'll be looking forward to meeting him. Oh, by the way James, he is a very good-looking guy, so keep your hands off of him. Joking of course.

The night before A.J. left for San Diego, he and David's passion boiled over with love. They had not been separated in all the months that they had been together. David's dependency on A.J. emotional support was the foundation for his newfound daily happiness that he had not had during his entire lifetime. He made A.J. promised to take every caution to be safe and to call upon King immediately if there was any inkling of danger. David knew that King and his cartel would protect him to the fullest. In fact, David called King to ask if he would send a couple of his thugs along with A.J. to be available, just in case. King agreed, Joie made a flight arrangement for A.J. and King's thugs to arrive in San Diego at nightfall two days later. James met A.J. at the dock where the seaplane landed. The two thugs disappeared into the night. James took "Arthur" to his personal residence where he lived alone. That evening they had drinks and had a casual conversation about nothing because Arthur, the name he is now using, revealed only he was from New Orleans of Creole descent.

His mother had left him abandoned on the streets at an early age, so he learned many skills to survive. James said you are exceptionally handsome, how old are you. 29, he replied.

What's the plan Author said? James said. Tomorrow I am sending you on a run to Montana with Michael, one of our most senior drivers, to make a delivery. It will take six days and when you get back, we can go over how the trip went and if you feel this is something you would like to do.

Okay, Author said, why don't you show me to my room? I am dead tired after my long trip; I need to get some rest. The next morning Author was introduced to Michael, the drugs were loaded in the secret compartments in the low-profile car and they took off on their six day trip to Montana. While on the road Michael asked Author question after question about his previous cartel experiences. He gave him complete lies based on his real-life adventures. They were so true sounding that Michael sounded envious of Author's past life and experiences.

When they arrived at their destination the drugs were exchanged for cash and Michael took the cash to a bank that the "Thunder Boys" used for their banking relationship which had branch banks all over the United States. He said excuse me; I need to deposit our cut of the transportation fee to our account and we take the rest back to San Diego to pay for the next shipment. Author asked, what is our cut? Michael said without knowing what was going on, 10%. Author said, what was the hall?" $250. 000..

Michael said. So, you are going to deposit $25,000. Yes, Michael said as he left the car and went into the bank.

When they got back to San Diego, Winston and King were there. They were enjoying a conversation with several of their cartel members that Winston had not seen for a very long time. James had ordered a lunch that had been delivered to their office and they were enjoying drinks and talking about Winston's newfound relationship with King of the infamous Jamaican Cartel. When Author walked into the office, he had a smile of relief on his face when he saw King and Winston.

After lunch was completed, Winston said, we are going back to our hotel to rest up and check out the luxury of its pool, so Author why don't you join us and then you can tell us about how you feel about my operation in San Diego. Sounds like a good idea, I need a rest after that long road trip. They all went to the Ritz Carlton, San Diego, where King had reserved a two-bedroom suite.

When A.J. walked in he said, this is beautiful. King, you didn't spare a dime for comfort, did you? King replied, we deserve only the best in life, my child. I have another surprise for you. Out walked David from the bedroom dressed in his swimsuit ready for the pool. A.J. ran over and kissed him as if for the first time in his life, What a wonderful surprise. You have made my day. He grabbed David by the arm and retreated to the bedroom, took a quick shower to wash off miles of road sweat, then pushed him into bed, stripping off his swimsuit. Revealing his hairy body, which turned

A.J. on like a light bulb. A.J. 's hairless black body was so beautiful to David's touch, they just exploded with passion.

King and Winston enjoyed the same sexual pleasure. Initiating the Ritz Carlton for the first time with passion and love of the most powerful cartel in the Caribbean Sea. After they were all finished messing up their bedrooms, they called for room service to change the sheets and they went to the pool for the remainder of the afternoon.

That evening Winston asked James to join them at the hotel for dinner. He arrived at 8:00pm sharp. Their formal dining room was grand. They were all dressed accordingly, and King introduced Author as A.J. as David's pardner and a member of their cartel on board the TITO V. Winston told James that A.J. was sent, under cover, to check out declining deposit receipts in his operations during the past two years. James was surprised that he was not informed but understood the reasoning.

A.J. said that Michael was to deposit $25,000.00 in their bank account in Montana after their delivery but instead the deposit was only $15,000.00. He skimmed $10,000.00 just on this one delivery. How many deliveries he has made over the past two years, he could have skimmed well over a million dollars. Winston's next question, James, why haven't you noticed this.

As they were finishing their meal James got up from the table and excused himself to go to the restroom. The rest of them finished their drinks. James was gone for an exceedingly long time, Winston got up and went to the restroom to check on him, he was nowhere to be found. When Winston returned to the table, he told King that James had left the restaurant and apparently knew more about the skimming issue than he let on. He had to deal with it right away. His entire San Diego operation was now in jeopardy.

King contacted the two thugs that he had sent to San Diego earlier to protect A.J., he told them to immediately go to Winston's office to locate James, that he had disappeared. If they locate him, keep him secure until they arrive. When the thugs arrived at the office James was there with Michael, who was stripped naked and tied to a chair in the back room. The thugs called Winston and told him that James was there with Michael and to come to the office immediately.

King told David and A.J. to return to suite and they went to Winston's office. When they arrived, it was just as if they were informed, Michael was naked tied to a chair and James had just begun verbally integrating him. James' interrogation techniques were not even mild as compared to the array of harsh interrogation procedures that King had used during his cartel lifetime. When Winston walked in, he looked at Michael in total disgust. A person that he had put his trust in for years screwed him out of millions. Winston turned to King, and said, will you handle this for me, this man has been part of my family for years, I just can't do it. King replied, I will take care of it, why don't you return to the hotel with David and A.J. I will be along shortly.

King told James to leave the room, this is going to be hard for you to take, I am sure. When James left, Michael spoke up and said, what are you going to do to me? King replied, get a million dollars out of your hide. King pulled up a chair right in front of him. His legs were stretched apart revealing his big balls and mighty uncircumcised Mexican cock His Mexican, hairless body, with thick black pubs surrounding his dick was tweaking just by the stare of King's eyes. He began sweating all over his body. King asked, for whom did you steal the money? Michael didn't say a word. I will repeat my question one last time, King said. Who did you steal the money for? Michael said, either way I am a dead person, so make it quick. King said, trust me

Michael, you are going to feel so much pain, that before I am done with you, you will wish you were dead.

Michael's body was extremely handsome. Those typed of bodies were the easiest to torture because of the person's vanity. King asked, have you ever thought about being circumcised? Never, Michael replied. King looked around the round and he found a knife, not the sharpest but it had a long blade. He took it and pulled back Michael's foreskin as far as he could. King said, I think I will use scissors instead of a knife to do this task. Fear was lurking in Michael's eyes. King made his first clip with the scissors., separating a big slice of his foreskin from his big dick.

Blood gushing all the way down Michael's balls dripping to the floor. Now ready for the next clip King asked. Who did you steal the money for, King asked. Still no reply. King took the second snip on his foreskin on the opposite side of his dick. Then King rolled back all his foreskin revealing the tender penis head all bloody. Michael was screaming out in agony; the pain was so severe that he was about to pass out when King threw a pan of cold water at his face to revive him.

Now King asked, who told you to steal the money? Michael was crying out in such pain that he couldn't talk plainly. He began stuttering, it was the Mexican cartel who we do business with.

They felt that our fees were too high, and they threatened the lives of my family still living in Mexico if I didn't steal the money. King asked, how do you pay them? They have a runner that comes to my home and pickles it up after each delivery. If anything holds up or interferes with the delivery they will execute my parents, brothers, and sisters living in Juarez.

You should have said that in the very beginning, your beautiful Mexican uncircumcised cock would still be in tack. Now we better get you to go to the clinic and get that cock taken care before you bleed to death. Well now you are circumcised, how do you like it? Michael replied, it looks shorter.

King left the room and went back to the hotel, leaving Michael in the hands of one of his fellow cartel members. When King got back to the hotel, Winston was waiting impatiently for him in the living room of the suite, with a drink in his hand. Well, what's the verdict Winston asked? King said, the long and short of it is he was being blackmailed by the cartel from Mexico that you are transporting drugs for. They are holding Michael's family hostage in Juarez. If he didn't deliver the kickbacks back to them, they would kill his family. How did you get that information, King? Well, let's say it was a bloody mess. His beautiful Mexican cock is now circumcised. King suggested that Winston put him out to pasture because he is no longer of service to your cartel. Michael and his family will just have to take their chances in Mexico.

TWO YEARS LATER

Their laundering business has exceeded all their expectations. Jaali & Assir ordered 20 more, fully trained "Executive-Service" teams from Kenya. The demand for personal protection in the islands had grown at such a rapid pace Adam found it difficult to keep up with the demand. They had increased their basic fee tenfold, and were cleaning thousands upon thousands of dollars daily, to the tune of millions of dollars monthly. Adam had a firm grasp on all 50 teams and there was a long waiting list of new clients for additional services.

Also, Adam had more than 200 individual security personnel assigned to shopping centers, private homes, and business all over the islands. The demand for that service was equally in demand and some of the more polished members from the Marquis Cartel were being utilized in this service.

Joie and Devin's transportation venue exploded in the first year of operation. Their perfectly painted and luxury planes were the only ones that VIP clients used exclusively to travel between islands and their private Caribbean homes. Joie ordered 11 more seaplanes and the same number of "go-boats" to provide for the increased requests that they received daily from their ever-expanding VIP clients. They also increased their fees 10-fold, and their business was a money washing machine for the cartel. A.J. kept a firm eye on every detail of the transportation hub. Always looking for new residences for the staff and seaplanes plus ensuring monies for fees were deposited in banks that David selected.

King suggested to David that they should buy additional yacht clubs on as many islands in the Caribbean as possible. That would give them the opportunity to launder more money and have additional dockages for any of their vessels. David asks A.J. to help him in the massive search. Only clubs on islands outside of U.S. control would be considered for purchase. After a 30-day extensive review, they identified twenty-five yacht clubs that were eligible for purchase. This time King asked Winston to negotiate their purchase. Winston was more than happy to take the lead and asked King how much money he should offer to purchase the clubs. King replied, however much it takes. Winston said, if they won't sell at any price, then what? King said, that is where I come in. Just let me know and I am sure they will sell.

One by one yacht clubs were purchased on numerous islands in the Caribbean. Some cost millions and some less. Twenty-two clubs were purchased in less than three months with only 3 that won't sell at any price which were on Aruba, Grenada, and Barbados. King was informed about their lack of interest in selling. King made a phone call to Bryan on Marquis Island and informed him that he needed help to persuade some owners of yacht clubs to part with their property, because he wanted to purchase them, and they refused to sell.

Bryan said, King, we went through this exercise a few years ago when we brought our current yacht clubs, didn't we? You are correct Bryan, so you know what to do. Bryan said, consider it done. Bryan said, would you have Joie send me a seaplane, it will be fast for my men to travel from island to island to wrap this up as quickly as possible. King turned to A.J. and told him to dispatch the airplane to Marquis Island immediately.

Bryan loaded six of his trusted cartel members on the plane and they landed on the islands in question.

The team paid a long and intense visit to each yacht club owner. Discussing with them the disadvantage of not selling their clubs. The four cartel members were very convincing. Their discussion resulted in each club owner placing a call to Winston accepting his offer for their club, now all 25 yacht clubs have been purchased. Staffing them with trust managers was the next issue.

King asked David about the management staff they should use on their newly purchased clubs. David said, let me think about that tonight. We are using all of the polished cartel members in our new companies which are generating a massive amount of clean money for us. I also know we can save money through the yacht clubs and the managers are very important. Let's meet in the morning, David said.

That night David and A.J. got back to their suite later than usual because they were working on details of their business responsibilities. When they walked in the room, they went straight to the shower to enjoy the soapy rub down that both of them had perfected since being together. After their shower, they put on their respective robes and preceded to the living area of the suite and sat arm in arm with their leg over each other's leg, enjoying the sexual beauty that each had to offer. The finest part of their relationship was the eye candy they enjoyed from their pardner, that always grew tasty each day they were together.

David told A.J. that they need 25 managers for the new yacht clubs that were newly purchased all over the Caribbean. A.J. asked if the clubs were a perfect place to launder money through? David said absolutely, but we need our man in charge to handle the deposit which we add additional funds to, just like our other business. Now the big question, where do we get their manpower? A.J. said from the Marquis Cartel. They have over 1000 men scattered around the islands and I am sure Bryan and Aaron know of 25 who are polished enough to manage these clubs. They don't have to be ghosts. Just trusted members of our cartel. In fact, I would suggest slowing down the revenue generated from the Marquis Cartel, because we are making so much clean money and have so much more money to clean, we don't need all of their revenue.

David said, that is a good idea. Let's meet together with King & Winston in the morning and present this idea to them and see what they think. Now my Polynesian beauty, David said, let's slide up our silk sheets and let our passion take us to the promised land again tonight. As always, they flew like on a magic carpet through the air, traveling softly and with an incredible amount of tenderness they achieved the ultimate sexual pleasure, then fell asleep, wrapped in each other's arms.

The next morning David and A.J. shared the plans they discussed the night before with King and Winston. King sat back in his chair and put his hands behind his head and gazed out the window at the blue water of the Pacific and said, what do you think about this idea Winston? Winston replied, ingenious. You two Winston said are a tactile thinking machine. Your idea is on target in both areas.

King put a call into Bryan and Aaron on his Island. He requested them to fly to the TITO V immediately and he would have Joie send a plane for them tomorrow morning. Bryan asks, what's going on? King said, we will discuss that when you get here. They arrived in Antigua at noon the next day and Simon picked them up from the dock with the armored limo and transported them to where the headquarters yacht was docked.

Bryan, Aaron, King, Winston, David, and A.J. all met in the man cave on the second level of the Ghost Ship. Chef Jeffery had prepared lunch for them and had it waiting for them when they arrived. While eating and having a drink, King went over the plan. First, he said, We need 25 of your finest and best looking cartel members to manage new yacht clubs that we just purchased around the islands. We are going to launder money through these locations and need a person loyal to our organization that can handle the bank deposits and keep the clubs under control. I am confident, out of the over 1000 men we have, there must be some handsome guys that would qualify for these positions. Aaron spoke up and said, our teams are in pairs, I am sure you know that, King. Well then send a pair to each location if that is what it takes. The question is, do you have 25 pairs that are polished enough to handle my request? We need them there as soon as possible.

Arron said, yes. Give me a week, I will bring them to our island and make sure they are polished up along with proper clothing, haircuts, and travel documents. I will send them their pictures for final approval by you and Simon and if they are okay, they will be on their way immediately. Okay. Now to the next request. We want to reduce the amount of money being generated by your cartel operation in the Caribbean. We can just wash more money than what we already have. How can we reduce your cash flow, King asked. Bryan asked, how much do you want us to reduce?

Frankly, Bryan, we don't need any of it. How can you stash it, King replied. Aaron said we have to give some thought to that. Do any of you guys have any suggestions?

A.J. spoke up and said, since you eliminated Little El Chapo in Panama, I am sure the rest of your clients are deathly afraid of you. Why don't you give them a three-month holiday from drug fees on their shipments with the understanding that it will resume when you choose. If any of them don't agree to the reinstatement, you will deal with them like you did with El Capo. Frankly speaking, you may not reinstate the fee for more than three months, which will be Kings and David's decision. During the time, the fees are being waived, give your cartel members time off to enjoy their well-earned wealth. We can provide them with transportation to other islands where we have business and some of them may want to join in on our new business ventures, you never know.

Bryan, you, and Aaron, can take the TITO IV on a long cruise around the islands and enjoy yourself. Rest up, you have both earned a well-deserved long holiday together. Don't put any contraband on board the yacht in case the authorities stop you. Bryan & Aaron stacked enough cash in yachts' secret compartments to pay for the voyage. King assured them that he would meet them at various yacht clubs that they own around the Caribbean. How does that sound, King asked. Bryan and Aaron spoke up at the same time and said, wonderful.

When Bryan and Aaron got back to their Island, they put the wheels in motion to fill the 25 yacht club manager positions. They identified cartel members from Jamaica and Puerto Rico that were the most handsome couples and relocated them to the mansion on Marquis Island. They had them take steam baths, oil their bodies with the expensive bath oils that King had left behind until they shined like a valuable coin. Clothing was sent in from Miami was very stylish. They received manicures to show off their smooth hands that were once used to execute their adversaries. In a week, they were ready for their assignment to the yacht clubs.

Bryan called King and told him all 25 couples had been readied for their assignment and to send planes for their departure at his convenience. King said he would send in two planes at a time and on each plane, he would have either David or A.J. go along to ensure that each couple got brief on how to handle bank deposits and that lodging was adequate. The planes made three trips a day so by the end of the week all of the newly acquired yacht clubs were fully staffed with a polished team of King's cartel managers.

David and A.J. both were shocked as to the handsome qualities of the men that Bryan and Aaron selected for the yacht club management positions. David, who was the only original leader of the Marquis Cartel, never knew the men that King had working for him. He thought to himself if these 25 were any examples of the rest of his cartel, King had surrounded himself with some really sexy men who, from time to time, he must have enjoyed.

David informed King that all the yacht club's managers have been assigned and within his and A.J. 's opinion, some really handsome men should be able to handle the club's operation.

The next thing on the agenda is to reduce the cash flow from their Caribbean operation. Bryan and Aaron split up their clients and told them the plan. Their clients were surprised but very grateful for the extra income that they would be receiving during its period of cancellation. It took about 10 days for all their clients to be notified as well as their cartel staff.

Lieutenant by lieutenant Bryan and Aaron notified them of the time off that they and their team would be enjoying for the next few months. Everyone had enough money to travel or stay in place to relax with their partners without the worry of any dangers. He also informed them that if they would like to travel to any of the island locations, they would make arrangements for their transportation. When this information was filtered down to the lowest couple in the cartel, they found it strange. Never during the years that they worked for King had he given them a break from enforcing his cartel's needs. Some of them didn't know what to do or how to act, being free from supervision from their leaders. Their lieutenants assured them that if they needed any assistance to feel safe to relax, to call upon them, they would help in any way possible.

So in the past two years, many changes took place. Millions upon millions of clean money has now been deposited in U.S. banks all over the world. David and A.J. had an accounting transfer system established that was so unique that no one but them could understand. With all their legal business running at 100% and at capacity, King was wondering what they should do next.

THE NEW TITO V

$\mathcal{K}$ing was sitting in the office and made a call to Capt. Oliver. He asked him how many hours were on the yacht and Oliver said 90,000. King said, isn't that a lot? Oliver said yes, it is time for a complete overhaul. King asked, how would you like a new TITO V for you and Wayne to be at the helm of? Oliver said, it would be an honor for us to take you and your team anywhere in the world. New yachts these days are so powerful and luxurious, you will not believe it. Oliver said I look at them frequently and I can't believe what they build. Okay, let me think about it, King said.

After he hung up the intercom. King put a call in to Jake at the shipbuilder in the Netherlands where they have purchased all of their yachts. He answered the phone on the first ring. He said, hello Jake, this is King, your longtime customer. Jake replied, well how in the hell are you? I haven't heard from you in a while. Well, my friend, we have been very busy and all of our yachts are streaming right along. Too bad you build them so good. What can I help you with, Jake asked. King said, my yacht has 90,000 hours on it, and I think it is time for a new one. Of course, a bigger and one more grand if you know what I mean. Jake said, how big?

King said, I don't know yet, what do you have? Jake said, King, you should come over and take a look at the three yachts that we have ready to go to the market. We are now putting the finishing touches on them, and they could cruise out of here anytime. How big are they, King asked? 275', and two 280'. Jake said, they are so beautiful that they will put your yacht to shame. You won't believe your eyes. King said, I think I will bring my pardner over and we will take a look at them. When can I expect you? I will have them in the water just in case you want to take any of them for a test drive. King said, I will also bring my captain and first officer. I don't navigate yachts. Make a reservation for two suites at the best hotel close to your facility, we will fly in tomorrow.

The next day Joie chartered a private jet for them to fly all four of them to the Netherlands. They landed in the early afternoon and Jake was waiting for them at the airport with a limo to take them to his office. As soon as they walked past the docks where the yachts were tied Capt. Oliver said, King, I told you the new ones were grand. King said, yes, I just can't believe my eyes. Winston spoke up and said, oh my god King, are you really thinking about buying one of these? King said, only if you like it. Winston said, what is there not to like.

King said, "Jake show us the 280' first". We might as well work our way down. Winston said, show us the master suite first, that is where we make all of our decisions, if you know what I mean. Jake took them to the first levels. When they walked in the room that extended forty' the entire beam of the yacht. It had a sliding glass door with a fold-out deck over the water, where they could enjoy their morning coffee or a private meal. The suite had two setting areas lavishly appointed with the finest silk fabric and the bed was larger than a king size. There were two baths. A jacuzzi in one and a waterfall shower for two, in the other. The flat screen TV covered one walk and an office area in another corner with two workstations.

There was room for 20 guests and 18 crew members, along with a very large Captains Quarters just off the bridge. A "Tree of Life" encircled the main staircase from top to bottom, hand carved out of Brazilian Mahogany. An elevator ran to every deck. A round dining room table under a stunning Venetian Glass Chandelier. In the main saloon there was a Baby Grand piano setting in one corner opposite the black carved mahogany bar. Their furniture was covered in the finest French silk fabric. The decks were all of the finest teak, and its haul was made of steel for North Atlantic crossings.

How about the engines, Oliver inquired. Jake said, the most powerful built, MTU 4200 HP, with a cruising speed of 16 knots and a range of 5,000 nautical miles. It is built for trans-Atlantic/Pacific crossings, with state-of-the-art surveillance & security systems far superior to their current TITO V.

King asked, how long would it take for you to have it painted out to our Ghost Ship specifications that you have on file. Jake said the exterior, three days. I would put my entire team on it. Right now, I don't have any other yachts under construction, so you have all my attention if you want to make a deal on this one.

Capt. Oliver said, I think we should take it out to sea and test those powerful engines and the rest of the new electronics installed on the yacht. I have to be trained in any new systems that are installed. OK, Jake said. Let's go up to the bridge, we have already prepared it for sea trials, we can take it out as long as you want. While we were out at sea, I had our chef prepare a lite lunch that we could enjoy on the aft deck, while we were under way. You will discover just how smooth it cruises at 16 knots. It is like riding on a magic carpet. Capt. Oliver and Wayne pulled it out of the harbor easily, using its four thrusters. When it cleared the dock and was in the main channel, Oliver headed out in open water.

When he cleared the last buoy marker, he increased the speed gradually until it reached its cruising speed. Oliver was impressed that there was a lot of power left if he chose to use it. The electronics on the vessel were just like Jake said, state-of-the-art. So massive they covered the entire bride window dashboard.

Oliver took every possible maneuver he could think of, including invasive techniques he had used several times during attacks by enemy aircraft and boats.

King and Winston enjoyed their meal. The dining room was so beautiful that it outshined the TITO V. The galley was state of the art with two of everything and room for three chefs and two Sous Chefs plus a cleaning staff. Every accommodation on the vessel was ultra-modern.

King took Winston by the hand and went below to the master suite. After they entered, he shut the door and took Winston in his arms and asked him, what do you think? Winston's reply, we deserve this. Let's make our final days together as beautiful as they can be. Let's cruise the world. Not just the Caribbean, we have outgrown that little hunk of sea. We have so much to do, and so little time left to do it. We are fortunate to be alive, with all of the shit we have done and been through. Let's buy it. Winston said. Okay, King replied.

Capt. Oliver docked the vessel easily, when they got back to port and King and Winston followed Jake to his office. Jake said, what's the price tag on this 280' luxury liner? Jake said, $250,000,000.00. Including the paint job. King said how about we take delivery with our crew here in the Netherlands in three weeks. I will bring you all cash when I pick it up. Oliver, do you need to stay and learn more about the inner workings of this mega yacht? Yes, that would be very helpful. You can take Wayne back with you to navigate the TITO V back to its final resting black until we decide what to do with it. Jake said, then do we have a deal? King said, put a sold sign on it.

That night they all check into the suites that Jake had reserved for them at the best hotel in town. When Oliver and Wayne got to their room, they went crazy with their manly assertive love that Oliver so tamed Wayne with. Wayne, even though he was so muscular, he let Oliver dominate him with his aged beauty, because there had never been a man in his life that had sexual satisfied him like Oliver. Wayne would respond in every way to Oliver's advances which made him melt like a teenager in heat.

Oliver loved Wayne, and never took issue with it. He was proud that he and Wayne were the masters of the best yacht for the biggest cartel in the world.

King and Winston, despite their ten years difference in age, were the supreme rulers of the sea and the cartel which they now ruled with passion. All their members were the best of the best and loyal to the King and David, its leaders. Who both sustained many hardships to guide their cartel from the jungles of Vietnam to the Caribbean, then to the South Pacific, and back to the Caribbean. They built an empire unmatched by anyone in the world of Cartels.

The next day King, Winston, A.J., and David boarded their chartered jet that was waiting for them and returned to Antigua and made preparations for the TITO V to voyage to Marquis Island, which or the last time would be its final resting place, while its crew readied themselves for their trip to the Netherlands, to board their new TITO V for a cruise to unknown destinations.

When the TITO V reached Marquis Island, it was docked permanently next to the TITO IV, over shattering its once stately beauty.

King had told Jake, the yacht's builder, to add an additional four crew members to the yacht because it would take that much to maintain it, due to its length and increased living capacity. And to provide him with their names immediately, so that Simon, head of security, could run background checks on them, prior to being employed.

All of their previous crew and cartel members wanted to be transferred to the new yacht, leaving the old TITO V, sitting at the Island crewless, until Bryan & Aaron could make arrangements to add whatever staff they chose, when the time came.

Joie readied a small, chartered Jet for the King, Winston, David, A.J. and the entire staff and cartel members, which totaled 32, to return to the Netherlands, Capt. Oliver added a 3rd Office, Chef Jeffery added a Sous Chef. Room Steward and Deck Staff were also increased by one. Jake provided all of the new staff, who were experienced yachters.

All 32 of them departed from Marquis Island, from the small runway, a week ahead of schedule. Scheduled to land in Amsterdam on the last of June. King had all of the cash tucked away on the plane to buy the new yacht. Their legal business was cleaning so much cash that their bank accounts were filled to capacity with spendable income.

Each account manager was completely in charge of their own business and required little to no supervision. King and David did not have any indication that their continued laundering operation or Cartel operation was in any danger of detection. The authorities from every county, including the United States, had them on their radar. Now there was a big "cash reward" for their capture. Bryan & Aaron retired on the Island, still pondering what or where they would go to enjoy their well-deserved retirement. They gave the entire security patrol time off.

The jet landed at Amsterdam airport seven days ahead of their scheduled arrival date. Five vans were standing by to transport them to the newly painted TITO V, docked at the shipyard. The new staff were waiting for them outfitted in their newly designed yacht uniforms, especially made by Jake, as a gift for King, his longtime customer. The uniforms were all black with silver, name decals embroidered on them. As usual the name of the yacht was not visible on the transom or any area of the vessel. Registration of the yacht was in

Spain, under an LLC that David had established several weeks ago after the planned purchase of the yacht.

Chef Jeffrey had the yacht's panties fully supplied and Capt. Oliver ensured that the fuel was topped off to its capacity for a 5,000-mile voyage to their next destination. All of the crew and cartel members were boarded, and the room stewards ensured that all were comfortably tucked away. David & A.J. walked into their new suite, suitcases in hand, just standing there for a moment to admire its splendor. When King & Winston arrived at their Master Suite, their personal items were being organized by the Room Steward from their luggage that had just arrived from the flight.

King called Jake to his office on board the new yacht. When Jake walked in, King asked him who had a seat in the extensive living area. He ordered drinks from the Steward and when they arrived, King expressed his personal gratitude for all of the fifteen years of great service that his company had provided him with. Just then Winston walked in with his drink in hand and sat next to King.

King got up from his chair and walked over to the desk and got the Louis Vuitton bag that was sitting there and gave it to Jake. When Jake opened it, there was the $250,000.00 in cash that they had agreed on for the purchase of the yacht. Jake said, I 'm sure I don't need to count it. King said, no you don't, just don't deposit it in any United States banks. Just deposit it in small amounts, in various accounts that you have, will you please. Jake said, not a problem. Jake said, now with the transaction signed, sealed, and now delivered, it is all yours. Where are you guys heading, Jake asked. King replied, we will decide that when we get out to sea.

Capt. Oliver at the controls, Wayne at the port thrusters, and Jack the new Third Officer, at the stern thrusters, the new TITO V pulled out of the port of Amsterdam, one of the largest ports on the Eastern European Coast. Then headed directly out to the Atlantic Sea, now turning South. After turning Capt. Oliver made a call in to King and requested their destination. King replied, reduce speed and I will get back to you.

King, Winston. David, & A.J., met in the office just behind the bridge on this vessel, to discuss where they would like to stop on their first voyage with the new "Ghost Ship." David suggested Spain, where he lived in exile while Jim, King's ex-lover and his love, was imprisoned many years ago. King called Capt. Oliver and said, Madrid, Spain. Oliver checked the new radar system and Madrid was only 1000 miles away. At their cruise speed of 16 knots, it was only a 54-hour trip down the Eastern European Coast. Capt. Oliver made an announcement over the ship's intercom, that they are setting course for Madrid and for everyone to enjoy their 54-hour voyage. Chef Jeffery along with Tommy and their new Sous Chef Jay started preparation for their first meal at sea.

Jack, the new 3rd Office, was previously the 1st officer on a 90' yacht for 3 years. Now as 3rd Officer, his duties are the ship's safety and maintenance which he was trained to perform. He was selected for the position over others by Jake, because of his experience, handsome qualities, and fitness that he had to handle the responsibilities of such a large vessel.

Jay, the new Sous Chef, was the Chef on the same yacht as Jack. Both of them were the same age of 30 and Jay was from Ethiopia and Jack, the 3rd Officer, was from Sudan, one of Ethiopia's bordering countries. Their friendship was not only cultural, but they had been isolated together on the small yacht for the last three years, as a result their friendship was deeply personal. They were assigned to the small crew quarters on the TITO V which made them very happy.

The round dining room table wood only seats 20 people. So, during meal periods some of the crew would take their meals in the crew mess, located in the galley. The elevator was used to transport food from the galley to the main dining room by 6 servers. During the first meal at sea, it was a practice run to organize the flow of food from the galley 3 decks below.

When they were 75 miles outside of Barcelona, King received a call from Bryan on Marquis Island. When he answered it, Bryan was extremely upset. He informed King that the DEA had just surrounded the compound and took custody of all the yachts and buildings on the island, and they had a search warrant for everything located there. King told him that there is nothing to find, so just cooperate with the authorities, do not show concern, and keep him posted after they complete their search.

Bryan told King that he and Aaron had over $2,000,000.00 in cash in their plane hangar on the other side of the island. They were hoping that the authorities had not discovered that location because it was well hidden in the jungle.

The DEA spent a day on the island scouring all the mansions, from top to bottom, for any money. They turned both yachts tied to the dock upside down, from bow to stern, finding no cash. The only valuable items they found on the island were furnishings in the main mansion and the splendor of both yachts tied to the dock. All three were of great value.

The authorities interrogated Bryan & Aaron for hours about their knowledge of the yachts and builds on the island. They informed the DEA that they were only caretakers on the island and showed them the titles to all of the property which was held in the LLC that David had established many years earlier. The lead investigator asked Bryan & Aaron both, who were the individuals named that was reflected on the LLC. They both played dumb and replied that they did not know. Bryan showed the investigator the bank statements reflecting regular deposits made each month, for expense money to maintain the islands and yachts docked on the pier.

The lead investigator took the bank statements, and they left the island under the cover of darkness. The mansion was ransacked, along with each yacht. The DEA did not go to the other side of the island where Bryan & Aaron had built a small airport and had their plane secured in a hanger painted in camouflage. As soon as the authorities left Bryan got on their golf cart and sped off to the hanger to check if their money was still there, and it was. Their plane and hangar were not discovered in the search, a fortunate break, they thought.

Aaron called King back the minute the authorities left the island. He was informed that the DEA found nothing of interest but did take the bank statements reflecting the monthly payments they receive to maintain the island. Aaron also informed King that Bryan's stash of $2 million in the hanger and their plane on the other side of the island, were not discovered.

King called David and Winston to the office and informed them of the raid on the island. The island had never been raided in all the years it had been in operation. David asked, what or who could be behind this raid? King called Simon to the office and asked him to investigate the reasoning behind the raid. Simon called GYS security in Miami, his former employer. In about three hours, he got a return call from GYS informing him that the authorities had received an anonymous tip, that a large amount of money was located on the island from cartel operations.

When Simon informed King about the tip, King asked if there was any way that he could find out where the call originated from?

Simon replied, that will take a little work. He called Adam, who was managing their security business in the Caribbean. He told Adam about the raid on the island and that an anonymous tip prompted the raid.

Adam said that he had a low-level connection with the DEA that he had worked with on a previous mission and that he would contact him and see if he could get any information.

Adam called Matthew, his DEA connection. Matthew was glad to hear from him as it had been several years since they had talked or seen one another. After pleasantries and small talk, Adam asks Matthew if he could do him a big favor, and he would need to keep it between them. Matthew said, sure, I would be glad to help you my friend, what is it you need? Adam said, your department raided an island just off of Miami, a week or so ago, and the raid originated from an anonymous tip. Can you find out where the tip originated from? Matthew said, that is right up my alley. I manage all the communication for the DEA. Incoming and outgoing phone numbers, etc. I know about that raid, we sent several agents to the island because we were expecting a big bust, at least according to the tip. The call came in from an unknown number in Amsterdam about three weeks ago. We were informed that there was a large movement of cash being transferred off that island.

The cash was from cartel operations in the Caribbean and South Pacific. Did the tip say to whom the cash belonged? Yes, Matthew said, and that there was a very large amount of cash. The DEA is giving a cash reward for any information leading to cartel convictions in the Caribbean because they had gotten out of hand this past couple of years, especially after El Chapo was killed.

How much is the reward, Adam asked. Matthew said, it all depends on the amount of cash recovered and cartel kingpins arrested. What we found strange was when we got there, the island was swept clean of cash and people. There were only two caretakers on that island. We found that very unusual based on the tip. Adam said, do you tape the calls, yes," Matthew said. Is there any way you can let me hear the tape? Hang on, I will pull it up and you can listen to it. In a minute Adam was listening to A.J.'s voice describing King's operations by name in the South Pacific and Caribbean. A.J. was also telling them about the vast amount of money hidden in the mansion and on the large yacht tied to the dock. A.J. also informed them that King & David were the leaders of the cartel and were traveling out of the United States territory. Adam told Matthew that they should get together and catch up on old times. Matthew agreed. Adam said that when it was convenient, he would send a plane for him and fly him to the Cayman's for a visit when he had the time. Matthew said, I will be looking forward to it.

THE PHONE CALL

*A*dam was stunned when he heard the information from Matthew's phone call. He sat down for a while to gather his thoughts on how to best communicate it to King, because he knew that when King heard it, King would explode like a nuclear bomb over the Atlantic Ocean. Adam had recorded the anonymous phone conversation that A.J. made to the DEA. The call was when King had just ordered the new TITO V in the Netherlands and before he was heading back to Antigua to take the old TITO V to Marquis Island for the last time. A.J. 's plan was for the DEA to catch all of them on Marquis Island, with billions of dollars in cash and arrest the entire Cartel kingpins, that he identified in the phone call, in one sweep of the island. A.J. wanted the maximum reward.

What went drastically wrong was that the DEA took over a month to put a crew together to raid the island. By the time they got there, King and the entire cartel had already departed, with all the cash, for the Netherlands, to pick up the new TITO V. A.J. was now sitting on pins and needles waiting for the other shoe to drop.

Adam made a call to King to report his findings about the raid on the island. When King got on the line, Adam said, who is in the office with you? King said David and I. Okay, Adam said. You guys better have a seat, I am going to play a tape recording of the anonymous phone call the DEA received to tip them off about the raid on Marquis Island. When King heard the recording, he knew instantly who it was. He looked at David who was crying in disbelief. David got up from his chair and went over to the couch to lie down, he was so weak that he could barely walk. He grabbed a trash can and emptied his stomach. King said, thank you Adam, you did a fine job, and we will get back to you as soon as we decide our next move.

King went over to the sofa and sat next to David to console him. David said, don't touch me. I am totally responsible for this entire situation. I am not worthy of your compassion. King replied.

David, over my lifetime, I have trusted many who turned out to be the wrong one and I had to deal with them, as I deal with any who cross me in the cartel world. This is no different. A.J. is a smooth talker. He used you to get into our organization. We knew that from the beginning, didn't we? King said, David you took a chance, and it paid off for a short period of time. You found passion didn't you, no matter how real or how false. I will handle A.J., don't you worry. David said, no I will handle A.J., that is my responsibility. I am the leader of this cartel, and if I don't demonstrate that I can lead, what am I, just a bookkeeper? King, I was in this cartel long before you got here and I plan to be here with you to the very end, which is our deal, do you understand? Yes, King replied.

David went down to Assir & Jaali's suite and knocked on the door. When they answered he asked them if he could come in and talk to them. They were honored to have David join them. David told them that he had a delicate situation, that he needed to be handled, and that he could use their help. Assir said, David you have the most powerful cartel member by your side now, why would you need our help? David said, this is something I screwed up and I need to handle it my way, so I want you two to help me.

You two are the best "Executive-Service" team that we have and that is what I need.

Jaali asks, what is the problem that is so great? David explained the entire A.J. situation to them and that they, along with the rest of the cartel, were almost arrested by the DEA on Marquis Island only weeks ago. Jaali & Assir were not as surprised as David had been. They said, once a trader always a trader, that's cartel law. Jaali asks, how would you like us to help you, David? We will be docking in Barcelona in a few hours. Its port is beautiful and mega yachts are everywhere. It is a party city for the rich and famous and A.J. has grown accustomed to the lifestyle that I have provided him.

I think it would be only fitting that he disappears among his peers. I thought that I would set him free for an evening with a pocketful of cash to explore the high-end party spots, I will rest up with plans to meet him later at the "W Hotel," a spot frequented by celebrities. I will never show up. Both of you will meet him there and his demise is your call, I don't want to see him or hear from him again, understood. Jaali & Aasir understood their mission and took only pleasure in bringing David's problem to a swift closure.

When they docked in Barcelona, they were surrounded by some of the most pristine yachts in the world. The TITO V, was by far a showcase on the pier where it was docked. People strolled by to admire its majestic lines and coloring. The crew took turns lining the deck in their silver embroidered uniforms, as if guarding the 280' yacht. Cartel members were now dressed in their finest to blend into the crowded streets in Barcelona.

That evening at about 7:00 P.M. Jaali & Assir departed the yacht for the hotel. They arrived an hour before A.J. was scheduled to check-in. They surveyed the grounds of the hotel and the many private villas surrounding it. They went to the front desk and made a reservation for David for an exclusive villa in the remote corner of the hotel grounds. The one that is usually reserved for movie stars or celebrities when they visit the hotel.

When A.J. arrived at the hotel, the doorman inquired if he had a reservation, and he informed them it was under his partner's name of "David." Hotel register was verified, and he was led to the remote villa. When he entered the spacious four room suite, clad in gold and silver, there was a note on the main table which read, "I will be back at 10:00PM". A.J. went to the bar and poured himself a Hennessy on the rocks and settled back into one of the lounge chairs on the veranda, overlooking the pool. The sky was so bright that night he could see downtown Barcelona. After he finished his second drink, there was a slight noise coming from the bedroom down the hall and he knew it must be David. He was nervous because no one, he thought, had any suspicion that he had tipped off the DEA as to the whereabouts of the cartel.

The veranda door opened and there stood Assir. A.J. said, what a pleasant surprise, in a shocked tone. Assir replied, I 'm sure it is. He said, David couldn't make it tonight and he asked Jaali and I to join you for the evening to keep you company, do you mind? A.J. replied, I have always heard Kenyan men are fun to be around, is that a fact Jaali said. Then, let's have some "black magic" fun.

Jaali & Assir stripped down to their black learn bodies where only their identical spears were ready to launch. Killing was a turn on for them and slow deaths were their specialty, especially when ordered to do so.

A.J. said, does David know what we are doing? Not in the least Jaali said, do you what to play A.J., Assir questioned? Hell yes, A.J. replied as he got up and threw his clothes on the floor revealing his elephant, which was getting larger, just by looking at the two black men. A&J went over to the gigantic bed and told A.J. to join them. He more than willingly got in the middle and grabbed both their swords. Wow, what power they have, A.J. said. I am sure that they could spear an elephant from afar. That's the plan Aasir said. A.J.'s skinny body was shaking from what he thought was going to be the anticipated pleasure of the spears piercing his body but just then Jaali flipped A.J. over and drew his long very sharp knife and said, "we have a big problem on our hands." A.J. said, "what is it? ''. They respond "YOU."

A.J. knew instantly that his cover had been blown. He went into defensive mode. I am sure we can work something out, can't we? A&J said I am sure we can. You fucked your way into the life of David and used his passion and trust to turn on our cartel. You little bastard, tonight you will never see the sunrise again. No matter how much noise you make, this villa is remote enough and I have it surrounded by several of our cartel members to take care of you after we are finished. Did you think that you would really get away with turning on the King of all cartels? If so, you are dumber than a black bitch from New Orleans.

Listen to me guys,' when I reported the tip to the DEA, A.J. said, the deal was David, and I would get immunity and be placed on "the witness protection program". Tell David about the deal, before you do anything else to me, please. Assir called David with the information. David said, hold everything, I will be down at the hotel in 30 minutes.

When David walked into the grand bungalow, he looked to his right, and there was A.J. spread eagle on the king size bed. David said, you always have a little string tied to your ass to save you from extension, don't you? I guess you can call it that, A.J. replied. You forgot about one thing that is the most important person in my life, **KING!** David bellowed. Your little string is tied to the wrong guy, David told him, while looking straight into his brown eyes.

For years King and I have protected you and provided you with a lifestyle of the Rich & Famous. Why would you turn us in for a small reward when you have access to billions? You have billions, A.J. said. Understand, during these years, I have never been given or received any payment for my contribution to the cartel, the $5 million dollar reward is a small payment for services. David with you by my side and both of us in the witness protection program, our life would be once and for all free from arrest and the cartel lifestyle.

David replied to the emotional cry of passion; A.J. you are not a faithful individual. From childhood to today, you are a selfish individual. Sorry to bust your bubble A.J. but you are not worth $5 million, and I could never live on land. I think we're making light of a serious situation here, David said. I came down here tonight, against my own better judgment, to ensure that you are taken care of, in cartel treason fashion. David left the room and shut the door behind him.

Jaali said, Assir spread his legs. A.J.'s hairless legs were kicking but Assir held them down without any trouble. Jaali tied his hands to the bed railings. Now A.J. was completely immobilized. First to go was his dreadlocks of which he was so proud. After they were removed, he looked like the negro that he was. The hair was shoved in his mouth but not enough to keep him from breathing because A&J wanted him to sound out the pain that they were going to inflict upon him.

They raised his legs over his head and tied his feet to the headboard. Now his asshole was revealed that he had used so many times before to gain information on their cartel. A&J stretched it so far open that blood was pouring out onto the sheets. They let it bleed for a long time. Then they removed each of his nipples, producing more blood. One by one they attacked the sexual spots of his body were removed, that he had used passionately on David to gain trust. A.J. was in so much agonizing pain that he knew that death was only a slice away.

Assir took the sharp knife and grabbed A.J. 's, now a very small elephant, and stretched it out as far as he could. Revealing its tip and slicing it off, then slowly removed each one of his little balls and laid them next to his face on the blood-stained sheet. A.J. was now blacking out from the pain and loss of blood. A&J let him lay there for the longest time, while they went to the bathroom to clean up and then to the veranda for a drink. Two hours later they walked out the door and told their cartel members to clean up the mess and dispose of the body. David's orders now complete, they returned to the TITO V for a drink.

David, who's composure was slowly being restored, sat with King and Winston in the Small Saloon of the TITO V. He was telling them that when he was in exile, while Jim was imprisoned, Barcelona was where he lived and worked. The city is so beautiful and richly populated that they could blend in very easily. All of their residents and yacht owners were monied, just like they were, and Spain did not have any reporting requirements on large currency transactions. The Port Vell Yacht Club was the oldest club in Barcelona, which dated back to the 4th century B.C. It had refitting facilities for mega yachts and could provide the finest in pantry supplies from fresh caviar to produce items that

Chef Jeffery and his cutlery staff could never provide the finest of meals, at a moment's notice.

David told King that he knew every street and alley in the city, where he worked as the assistant to one of its wealthiest residents. King suggested that they contact Bryan and Aaron on Marquis Island and have them join them in Port Vell, since the island is now under surveillance by the DEA. David thought that was a good idea, so King placed a call to them.

When Aaron answered, he was surprised to hear about the invention to Spain. He asked King, what should they do with the remainder of his cartel operation in the Caribbean? Close it down, was his reply. When you get here, we will discuss the plan.

David placed a call to Joie to ready a small jet to land on the island immediately. They are picking up Bryan and Aaron and taking them to Little Cayman. When they boarded a larger jet for their trip to Madrid, when they arrived, they caught a shuttle to Port Vell, where the Ghost Ship was docked. King and David welcomed them with open arms. After everyone had arrived, King made a general announcement that there would be a mass meeting, on the aft deck, in 10 minutes.

Cannes, France will be our next stop, King announced. Capt. Oliver called ahead and secured a 300' docking at the Vieux Port de Vannes Yacht Club, which flaunted the Millionaire and Billionaire lifestyle, with mega yachts but none matching the elegance of the Ghost Ship. Cannes Film Festival had concluded two months earlier but there were telltale signs of it everywhere you went. This richly populated city on the French Riviera is lined with sandy beaches, upmarket boutiques, and palatial hotels. The TITO V, stood out as the prime mega yacht and its pristine beauty along with its crew, were the standout at the Yacht Club.

While docked in Cannes, two pairs of the cartel members disembarked the Ghost Ship for a leisurely walk along the pier to ensure security was in place, and to take in the sights of the very small town. Two of Kings and David's security detail always remain on board, always, to provide for their personal protection. They planned for only a short stop in Canines, before their voyage to Portofino, located on the exquisite Italian Riviera.

There was no dockage in Portofino, only anchorage in its beauty bay, surrounded by the postcard paintings of the homes built on the hills surrounding the harbor. After the bow and stern lines were set on the Ghost Ship, it was just nightfall. The reflective underwater lights of the yacht made it look like the "Black Ghost" that it was, envious to all of those in Portofino.

For Several weeks now King and David have been planning for the final closure of their long and successful cartel operation. That actual closing was one issue, but the emotional closure of their long relationship together was one that they had not given much thought.

King and David were so emotionally bonded by the cartel that eliminating it was like cutting the ambilocal cord between them. Jim, King's first love, and David's first love, bound Jim & King together when Jim succumbed to cancer several years ago. Since that time King has taken care of David as if he was his own son.

Their common bond was the cartel, how would their new life be without the constant tread of cartel operations?

The elimination of David's lover was another void left to fill in David's life. And one that he never had to contemplate before. David had found passion for the very first time in his life. King could not fill that void. But King had found a new life pardner with Winston. The Leaders of the once most powerful cartel were both filled with passion rather than the desire to kill or defend their cartel.

King and David sat for hours in the office of the Ghost Ship talking about their past lives together and what each wanted for their future. King assured David that he had found his "mate for life."

David was not content any longer with being alone. He was open to allowing another person into his life. King's only request was that he approve of David's' next companion. David agreed.

After they toured the small port city of Portofino, they sent a course to Sicily. The island is historically the world's best preserved example of Greek and Roman temples, art, and miles of beautiful coastline and beaches. Sicilian connection to the Mafia is widely known in United States history. That connection was one that King wanted to explore while visiting the island. He asked Jaali & Assir to join him and David in the office of the Ghost Ship. Their best "Executive-Service" team was challenged to infiltrate the city and gain as much knowledge as possible about mafia life and culture on this small island.

While docked at the Yacht Club in Palermo, the capital of Sicily, Jaa; I & Assir slipped into town to run with the bulls, one should say. Their training was so smooth that they could attend any function or enter any establishment without notice to gain any information. While the vessel was docked, they made several trips into the city, each time gaining more insight into the small mafia still based there.

During their fourth trip into town, they were at a small bar in the lesser part of town, and met a guy who's name was Augusto, a Portuguese, who arrived two days ago. He said that he was sent here from Miami to meet a person, at this bar, to connect his organization with some muscle. Augusto enquired, if Assir & Jaali were his connect? So, the connection was made!

Assir & Jaali called King from the bar. Informed him about the connection and asked him what he wanted them to do. King said, I got one hell of an idea. **We need Miami**, Bring Augusto to me now. Augusto arrived at 2pm, joining everyone in the Small Saloon, on the Ghost Ship. Needless to say, Augusto was ready to shit his pants. A round of drinks was ordered, and the mafia needs in Miami discussed.

Introductions concluded, all relaxed as one can be, business began. King was only curious about the Miami gang that needed muscle. Angusto poured out all the problems that their gang was having with the ever-expanding Haitian Cartel. King asked, how much muscle do you need? Angusto replied, depending on how skilled they are. The seed planted… **The New Cartel.**

THE NEW CARTEL

$\mathcal{K}$ing and David had put Adam in charge of running all of the legal operations in the Caribbean. It was cleaning millions upon millions of dollars a month which were deposited in local bank accounts that David had established in numerous banks in the Caribbean.

The business was operating flawlessly. Joie & Devin's Transportation Business had now grown to thirty plans, and they booked weeks in advance. Adam's Security Business was assigned to all islands and the Executive-Service details were so in demand that he had to recruit additional members from Kenya.

King and David sat down with Aaron and Bryan to plan the closure of their entire Caribbean Cartel operation. First of all, they did not need or want any more cash receipts from their operation. Its operation was the greatest exposure David and King had to the authorities. How to close it was a big mystery. King said, with the new business deal we have with Italians in Miami, let's get all the Lieutenants together and offer them that contract. The phone call made, details, numbers, dollars, and most of all, it was all there's. King and David's parting gift to their former Cartel.

Over 920 members of King's previous Jamaican Cartel were dispatched to Miami. Some groups were as small as 20 and some as large as 250. The men and their partners were proud of who they were and the years that they served the King of Cartels, with undying loyalty. Now they together were the **New Jamaican Cartel.**

In summary, Marquis Island, both yachts, and the small plane were abandoned. The business locations in the South Pacific sat empty. Nothing left of the former Marquis Cartel could be seized by the authorities because not one member was assigned to any of its locations. The former members of the cartel, who were left, were on board the TITO V, cruising the Mediterranean Sea.

A miracle happened when they anchored at the Greek Island of Crete. David, all by his lonesome, went strolling on the island's promenade. During his stroll he met a very handsome slightly older man. Let's say, 7 years older. He was olive colored in complexion. Black hair, 3" taller than David who is 5'11", and medium built.

David had lunch with Robert who was from New York. He was on holiday, and this was his second day on the island.

During lunch after all pleasantries passed, they made a date to have dinner on board the yacht that evening. David told Robert that he would arrange for a shore boat to pick him up at 7:30pm at the dock. Dress for the evening was. relaxed-informal. Robert arrived in the Main Saloon of the Ghost Ship, totally at ease. King was first to stand and welcome him on board. Winston followed suit. Robert was so nonchalant; Winston questioned his relaxed body language in his mind.

Finally, after the third drink, even David had two drinks. King asked Robert, where do you hail from and what do you do? Robert smiled and said, "I hail from California, and I am a Trust Fund Child '', never worked a day in my life. Being from the "Foster '' family, the Railroad and Banking ones. You wear it well, King replied. Robert inquired the same. David spoke up this time. All of us on this yacht are retired, I am sure that sums it up. We hit gold in several locations around the world. The Ghost Ship, as we call it, is our home. Robert said, your home is pretty grand.

David warmed up to Robert quickly. David liked the feeling of security that Robert age provided. Robert was not looking for a mate, as he always avoided people looking for money or to be kept. Robert said to himself, this guy is totally different, he may be a keeper. The evening's dinner was another one of Chef Jeffery's culinary delights. Twelve o'clock was striking on the ship's clock when Robert said, I guess it is time for me to go.

David said, spend the night in one of our spacious suites. I will have a Steward show you to your room and everything fresh, will be waiting for you.

The next morning David, Winston, King, Bryan, and Aaron were sitting around the dining table in the Small Saloon. Robert walked in, freshly showered and smelling of the yacht's cologne. He said, two new faces. David said, this is Bryan & Aaron, who are also retired with us. Robert said, it appears that we have the heads of the cartel around this table. King's eyes lit up. He stood up and without a blink of his eye or a breath said…. "You are absolutely right." We are the former leaders of the "Marquis Cartel." You're famous, Robert said. In banking circles, your cartel comes up as much as the biggest Mexican cartels, as experts in money laundering.

I don't believe anyone could have told me that I would meet you, David, on a sidewalk in Crete. What in the hell do I do now? It's like Bonnie & Clyde, Robert said. Shit, I like you David, and you just as you are. What are we going to do about it?

The very next day, Robert moved into the suite next to David's on the Ghost Ship. Capt. Oliver now has the yacht chartered for an 1800-mile cruise to Morocco. During the days at sea, and the many weeks thereafter, David and Robert shared their time to get to know one another. Their friendship grew, and so did their passion for one another. Once again David found that perfect companion. They are both "Living Off Trust Funds."

King and Winston are an interesting pair. About the same size and of handsome qualities. The slight age span makes them seem like cousins or nephews/ uncles. They are not gay appearing in any way. Frankly speaking, they can both make you walk like a duck for two weeks, guaranteed. King, the one o' powerful. He towered over 1000 of his Jamaican Gang. Then took over the Marquis Cartel and empowered it. Expanding into the "South Pacific Islands and The Kingdom of Tonga". King and David will make the decision to retire for the final time.

The Marquis Cartel's operations have been put to rest with **passion**, instead of a hail of bullets. Its business life had been extinguished, as fast as with a

"Viet Cong Rocket ", like in the very start of our cartel love story, in Vietnam.

The Cartel did not close slowly and painfully as an individual who commits an act of "Cartel Treason." Those treasonous people not only leave their gang behind, but hurt emotions and oftentimes false passion, so painful, a person could carry the scares for a lifetime.

Luycer says,

"I hope that I have shared with you the exciting conclusion of King, David, and their cartel. I am honored to say; I am King's proctor and have been for over 40 years. No harm will come to King while under my protection, I will also keep a watchful eye on Winston, David, now Robert too, along with the rest of their security staff and crew. While they safely housed on their **Ghost Ship,** cruising the oceans afar.

The Last Voyage of The Ghost Cartel

The End

Disclaimer To the Book

This is a work of Adult Fiction. Names, places, characters, business, events, and intense are the product of the author's imagination. Any resemblance to actual persons living or dead, or actual events is purely accidental

References: Wikipedia

ABOUT THE AUTHOR

*J*ames was born the son of sharecroppers and grew up in tenement housing on a farm in Iroquois County, Illinois. At the age of thirteen, he and his family moved to a small village in the same county where he graduated high school. At the age of eighteen, he moved from the small village to Champaign, Illinois, the home of the University of Illinois, and secured a position as a teller at one of the major banks. Because of his "Personality, Looks, and Communication Skills," it was not long before he was promoted to Head Teller. During this time, he was drafted into the Army to supplement the surge of troops during the Vietnamese crisis.

His distinguished military career was recognized when he received a Bronze Star Medal. His training in the Army prepared him to pursue his life's dream of acquiring financial freedom. After he was discharged from the Army, he returned to the small Illinois bank and discovered it had limited promotional opportunities for him to achieve his dream.

James sought and obtained a position with the world's largest banks based in California, where he spent twenty-five years. During this time, he worked internationally in fifteen different countries around the world. Additionally, he was recognized as the bank's top motivational speaker. After spending ten years overseas, he was invited to join the Chief Executive Officer of

International Operations as his personal attaché. He served in this position for five years. During that time, he supervised all the Bank's International Operations Centers with the highest degree of efficiency.

Upon completing this assignment, he served ten years as the Regional Vice President of Operations for Northern California. After which, he retired at the age of forty-five. Upon retirement, he spent several months on his yacht named "*The Jim Marquis*" until he relocated to Key West, Florida. After several years he relocated to his Lake House in the Upper Peninsula (UP) of Michigan and enjoyed the tranquility that only remoteness can provide. After a decade and tired of the snowy cold winters, he relocated to southern Texas for another decade. In 2019, he returned home to Sacramento, California. Where he chose to reside in one of his family's homes.

While watching all the movies that television could provide during the pandemic, he wrote his first book, "*1862 A Civil War Love Story*", in which he visualized "Michael B. Jordan" as the lead character. "*1862*" is the forbidden love story that involves Confederate Soldiers, plantation workers and a couple of rednecks from Kentucky during the waning years of the civil war. Since its release, the story has received 5-star reviews.

The book's writing was influenced by the storyline of *"Brokeback Mountain.* "*1862*" is a compelling inter-racial gay novel far exceeding the love between men as characterized in *"Brokeback Mountain."*

He continued to write six more books in a cartel series of international intrigue, drugs, imprisonment, success, and failure, and of course love and passion.

The first book, *1968 A Vietnam Love Story,* was influenced by his own personal events before, during, and after his tour of duty in

Vietnam. This book goes into the emotional side of war. The main character takes you on that journey which lasted over two decades with love found, lost, and found again. Introducing you to the world of high finance in which multibillion dollar business decisions are made on an international scale and introduces the reader to the *"Cartel World."*

In his next novels, he continues to build cartel action and suspense. *"The Marquis Cartel, The Revenge of the Marquis Cartel, Ghost Cartel,* and *Last Voyage of the Ghost Cartel,"* take you through three decades of unbelievable adventure to form the largest gay cartel in the world. Evasion from the authorities and making and cleaning billions in cash was their goal. The reader is shown the path traveled by the *King* and his associate *David's strategy* to build the biggest cartel in the Caribbean, South Pacific, and to retire with billions, without detection from the DEA, FBI, or other federal agencies.

A collection of over 1000 Jamaican Thugs, and specialized teams from *Kenya* all pledged their life to the Cartel, then to their partner, and fought to the death to complete the Cartel's mission. *King,* the leader of the cartel, has unique skills and lifestyle that ensures the safety and passion of its members are secure.

James is continually challenged to create suspense, mysterious killings, sexual intrigue, passion, and love in all of his novels. These novels have brought recognition to James as an inspiring new author who dares to be himself.